Critical Acclaim for Romesh Gunesekera's *Reef*
Finalist for the 1994 Booker Prize
Nominated for the 1995 New Voice Award

"Epic...a breathtakingly simple and elegant book that also manages to astonish."

—*Details*

"An enchanting, endlessly funny and affecting novel...truly exquisite. You could travel round the world and not be so transported to another place, to a heartbreaking, exotic island, to the turning tide of history and yet at the same time to the timeliness of nature, love and devoted friendship, as you will be with *Reef*."

—*San Francisco Chronicle*

"Rich in sensuous descriptions...Gunesekera's powerful novel is peopled with colorful, memorable characters. Mr. Gunesekera, a master storyteller, writes about them with great affection, casting a spell of nostalgia with his lyrical prose."

—*New York Times Book Review*

"Romesh Gunesekera writes with easy delight in *Reef*...He is a reminder that some of the most interesting and finely wrought fiction in English now comes from South Asia."

—*The London Observer*

"A book which touches powerfully and deeply."

—*The Times* (London)

"This beguiling first novel serves up a lot of sensuous language and lush images as it chronicles the growth of a Sri Lankan houseboy who watches his little island slowly deteriorate into something rather hellish...It's hard not to feel moved."

—*Cleveland Plain Dealer*

Romesh Gunesekera

Monkfish Moon

Riverhead Books, New York

Riverhead Books
Published by The Berkley Publishing Group
200 Madison Avenue
New York, New York 10016

Copyright © 1992 by Romesh Gunesekera
Cover design by James R. Harris
Cover art: Ivan Peries, *Moonlight*, undated, unsigned, oil on
board, 59 x 29cm.

First published in Great Britain by Granta Books 1992
Published in hardcover in the United States by The New Press,
New York
First Riverhead edition: July 1996

The Putnam Berkley World Wide Web site address is
http://www.berkley.com

Library of Congress Cataloging-in-Publication Data

Gunesekera, Romesh.
    Monkfish moon / Romesh Gunesekera.—1st Riverhead ed.
      p. cm.
    ISBN 1-57322-550-9
      1. Sri Lanka—Social life and customs—Fiction.   I. Title.
PR9440.9.G86M64   1996
823—dc20   95-47305
                                      CIP

Printed in the United States of America

10 9 8 7 6 5 4 3 2 1

*For my mother and my father
the untold story
and Helen*

There are no monkfish in the ocean around Sri Lanka

Contents

A House in the Country

THE NIGHTS HAD always been noisy: frogs, drums, bottles, dogs barking at the moon. Then one evening there was silence. Ray stepped out on to the veranda. There was no wind. He pulled up a cane chair and sat down. The fireflies had disappeared. The trees and bushes in the small garden were still. Only the stars above moved, pulsing in the sky.

These were troubled times in Sri Lanka, people said, but nothing had happened in his neighbourhood. Nothing until this surprising silence. Even that, he thought, may not be new. He was becoming slow at noticing things.

Then a shadow moved. A young man appeared, his white sarong glowing in the moonlight.

He was much younger than Ray. Not as tall, but stronger, smoother skinned. His eyes were bright and hard like marbles. He came and stood by a pillar. A moth flew above him towards a wall light.

'What has happened?' Ray asked, looking around.

Siri scratched his head, gently rocking it. 'Don't know.'

'There's not a sound.' They spoke in slow Sinhala.

Ray liked this extraordinary silence. He liked the way their few words burst out, and then hung in the air

11

before melting. It was the silence of his winter England transplanted. The silence of windows and doors closed against the cold. Lately Colombo had become too noisy. He had never expected such peace would come so close to war.

'The radio?' Ray asked. Siri always had a radio on somewhere in the house droning public service. 'Radio is not on?'

Siri shook his head. 'No batteries.' He bit the edge of his lower lip. 'I forgot to buy new ones. Shall I go now?'

It was late: nearly eleven at night. The little shop at the top of the road would have closed. Ray felt uneasy about Siri going too far. 'No. Go tomorrow. Better than now.'

Siri nodded. 'Too quiet. Maybe another curfew?'

But it was not simply the silence of curfew. There seemed to be no sound at all. In the two years Ray had been back in the country there had been many curfews. They had lost their significance. Only the occasional twenty-four-hour curfew had any impact. Even those rarely inconvenienced him; he was often content to stay in his house.

But in recent months there had been a new wall to build, shutters to fix. Each day had been shattered by hammer blows aimed at protecting his future privacy. Ray had taken to escaping to a bar off Galle Road; it made him more than usually melancholic.

'Didn't you go out at all today?' Ray asked.

'These shutters,' Siri pointed inside. 'I wanted to finish the staining . . . '

'Good. They are very good.' The wood had the perfume of a boudoir.

'I was working on that, the last coat. Finished about seven-thirty. And then, when I was listening after my bath, the radio stopped.' He twisted his fingers to show a collapse into chaos. 'I didn't go out then because I thought you would be coming home soon.' His face widened in an eager smile.

Ray looked away. His long shadow danced down the steps. A gecko twitched. Ray had come home late.

Siri shifted his weight and moved away from the wall. He sat on the edge of a step. 'What do you think they'll do, Sir?'

'Who?'

'Government.'

Ray leaned back in his chair with both hands clasped behind his head and stared up at the night sky. He saw only a waning red moon. 'I don't know. What do you think?'

Siri rubbed his thighs. He'd heard people say they should hold elections—the government might even win; but people also said that there probably wouldn't be any elections. They'd try another 'military solution' against the JVP—the People's Liberation Front—like against the Tigers, and get stuck with war.

'Trouble is no one knows.' Siri's mouth turned down at both ends, but his was not a face that could show much distress. 'Nobody really cares, do they? Except for themselves.'

Ray put his hands together, matching fingertips, and half nodded. 'Not many people do.'

Ray had not planned on having any help or company when he first returned to Colombo from England. He'd had a secure job with a building society, a flat in London, a car, and a happy circle of acquaintances. There had also been a woman he'd spend a night or two with from time to time. But they never had much to talk about and quite often he simply thought about going back to Sri Lanka. One summer she went back home to Ulster; she

13

got married.

That year he too decided he would go back home. He resigned from his job, sold his flat and left. The business of moving absorbed his energies, and he had no time to think. He had a house left to him in Colombo and money saved over the years. He hoped he would find out what he wanted once he had freed himself from the constraints of his London life, and once he had retrieved his past.

The first time he saw the house his uncle had left him, his blood turned to sand. It looked like a concrete box shoved into a hole. Nothing of the elegance of his converted London flat, nor the sensuality of the open tropical houses of his Sri Lankan childhood. But then he found Siri.

It was the luck of a moment. Ray was with a friend at a bar. They were drinking beer. His friend asked about the house, and Ray said he had too much to do. He needed builders, renovators. His friend mentioned Sirisena, Siri, who had done their house.

A few days later Siri turned up. Ray liked his quiet competence; the strange innocence in his eyes. He didn't quite know how to develop their working relationship. To him it should have been simply a relationship of employment. The old conventions of Colombo serfdom died years ago, but Siri kept saying 'Sir' and circumscribing their roles. He developed his job from artisan, to supervisor, to cook, night-watchman and, in effect, the servant. Ray felt things had to change incrementally: he acquiesced and played the roles Siri expected. Siri himself was too deep in this world of manners to feel the pull of revolution being preached across the country.

Siri did the carpentry, found the plumbers, the electricians. He moved in and slowly rebuilt the old

14

house around Ray. Walls were replastered, doors rehung, floors tiled. And he kept the house in order.

Although in England Ray had done many of these things himself, here he found he needed Siri. Much of the renovation was straightforward, but from time to time he would see the need for change. He would talk it over with Siri, his fingers designing in the air. The next day Siri would start on the work.

In this way a new veranda was created; rooms divided. The curfews allowed him to examine progress. They provided the snapshots when activity was suspended. The workmen didn't come; it was only Ray and Siri.

It was the first time since childhood that Ray had had a constant companion. He encouraged Siri to talk and wished, in a way, that Siri could turn into his confidant. He wanted to ask, 'Why do you treat me like a . . . ' but could never bring himself even to suggest he saw himself as a master. Siri simply showed respect in his antiquated fashion.

Ray's only response was to care. He didn't know how to respect in turn, but he felt a need to protect in a way he had never felt before. He tried to be generous with the pay and reasonable in his demands, but Siri seemed to want to do everything that needed doing and to spend all his time in the house. He hardly ever went back home to his village.

When Ray bought furniture for Siri's room, Siri looked dismayed.

'What's wrong?'

'I don't need all this.' Siri pointed at the cupboard and the new bed, the new pillow and mats.

'Some comfort won't harm.'

'I have nothing to put in the cupboard. The old bed was fine, just as it was.'

Ray said now that Siri had a steady job he might

accumulate some possessions.

'What for? My family need things, my mother, my brother. I only need something to do. Some place . . . Sir, this house I am making for you. It will be beautiful. To me that is enough.'

Ray didn't know what to do. He was embarrassed and puzzled. He pulled down his chin and snorted, like a bull backing out of a shed. The early days were confusing. Siri seemed exhilarated by the freedom he had to use any material he desired to turn ideas into reality, even his own ideas. He had never been given such complete responsibility before. Ray didn't understand this. It took time for him to see Siri as himself.

That night, that silent night, back in his room Ray kept thinking about Siri. He felt uncomfortable. He would have liked to have talked some more. To have said something to Siri that would have helped them both understand what was happening. Instead they had sat there swallowing silence.

The next morning Ray woke to the scream of parrots circling the mango tree in the garden. He dressed quietly and stepped into the soft rubber of his shoes. In fifteen minutes he was out of the house.

The road was deserted. He walked to the end and crossed over into the park. He had a route he could follow with his eyes closed, carefully planned and timed to avoid other people.

He liked walking alone, in control of the sound around him: the thud of his feet, the blood in his ears.

The sky that morning was grey. Large, heavy clouds rippled overhead. Crows crowded the flame tree by the main road. Bats hung on the telephone lines.

Usually Ray walked for about twenty minutes. On his

way back he would collect a newspaper from the small general store near the temple. Then at home he would savour a pot of tea and read the news. This morning he was looking forward to returning to an almost completed veranda.

Siri would have prepared the tea and disappeared: a tray with a white cloth, a small blue Chinese tea pot filled to the brim and protected by a embroidered tea-cosy, one plain white cup and saucer, a silver jug of boiled milk. A silver spoon. Ray would normally find the tray on a glass table. He had learned to accept this service as a part of life. He no longer resisted it and he never did the same for Siri. He never went that far.

But sometimes, in the evening, he'd offer Siri a drink. He would find Siri sitting on the steps or stalking about the garden.

'Have a beer?' he'd say.

Siri would nod hesitantly and approach Ray smoothing his sarong. He would take the glass and sip slowly. He never sat down when he had a beer. He would stand while Ray sat. Whether they shared a beer or not, Siri was usually quite happy to talk. He'd tell Ray about life in the village: river bathing, family feuds, someone running amok. In the middle of such a story, Siri would sometimes stop and peer at Ray. 'Why do you look so sad?' he'd ask, and surprise Ray with his directness.

One evening Ray asked, 'Have you built your own house?'

Siri's mouth wrinkled; he slowly shook his head. 'No. Not my own. I have no land.'

'What about the family farm?'

'It's very small. We have one field.'

His father had tried milch cows, but couldn't compete with the local MP's people. They had commanded everything until the JVP moved in. By then the cows had

17

dried up and Siri's father died. His brother stayed to work the one field, but Siri left.

'Could you ever go back to live in the country again? Now, after a city life. After what you've learned.' Ray wanted to know how genuine his own feeling of returning to roots was. He knew it was never possible to go back to exactly the same things, but at the same time he felt the old world never quite passes away. Suddenly the frame shifts and you find yourself back where you started.

'Go back to the country? Village life?' Siri smiled like a little boy thinking about the ripeness of mangoes. 'Yes. Yes, I could go back to a life in the country. Like my brother's. If there was a house like this in the country.'

'Maybe you should start saving some money?'

Siri found this suggestion amusing. 'There's never been the chance.' He clicked his tongue and added, 'Until now.'

The next day Ray went with Siri to the National Savings Bank and got him a savings book. He arranged for a part of Siri's salary to go straight into savings. But even after that Ray felt Siri was still not thinking far enough ahead. He was going to lose out. It troubled him at the time, although his own concern about Siri puzzled him more.

Months later Ray heard that some private land was being sold close to Siri's village. He asked him about it.

'No, Sir, I didn't know.'

Ray took a piece of paper from his pocket and unfolded it. 'Look, this is what it says.' He described the position of the land. It was near the coast.

'Yes,' Siri nodded. He knew the area.

'That land is a good price, I'm told.'

'I don't know, Sir. But there's not much growing there.' He delicately licked his thumb and forefinger, 'You can taste the salt in the air there.'

'No, it is good land. You can grow cinnamon or

18

cardamom. Something like that. I know Mr Wijesena has some land there.'

Siri nodded. 'He has grown some cloves I think. Are you thinking of buying some land also?'

Ray was standing by the door. He took a deep breath. Suddenly he realized he was nervous. Sweat ran down his back. Things were not very clear in his head. He had started talking about the land with the simple intention of planting a seed in Siri's mind: land was sometimes available. He had probably hoped, he now thought as he stood there, that Siri would connect the idea of his savings with the possibility of a piece of land out in the country. But as they talked he realized that it would take Siri years to get a living out of such land. That Siri's life would be, at best, only a life of subsistence. He would sink into the earth, unless something radical could be done.

'I was thinking about a piece of land,' he said, looking down, away from Siri. 'I was thinking about you.'

'Me?'

'Maybe you should take some land.'

'Impossible, Sir. Even with the savings you arranged. Good land in our area is expensive.'

'I know. But if you could, would you like some land? Is it what you want?'

'You know me, Sir. I like to build. I like to grow. With some land there I can do both. And I can do as I please.'

'But when?'

'When my luck comes. When the gods take pity.'

'I can lend you the money,' Ray said quietly. It was not exactly what he wanted to say. The words slipped out like moonlight when the clouds move.

'But then I will be a debtor. I could never pay it back.'

Ray could see that. It could be the rut in the ground one never got out of. But he had a plan working itself out as he spoke.

'I'll buy the land. I'll *give* you a portion. You for your part can plant the trees for us both. Cinnamon, or *cadju* or whatever.'

Siri's eyes brightened. There was a slight smile playing around his lips. The smooth boyish cheeks rippled. 'Why, Sir? Why do you want to do this for me?'

Ray could say nothing except that he wanted to.

'You are good Sir, very good.'

Ray made arrangements to buy the land. He felt better for it. He had followed his instincts. But his instincts had changed. They were not the fine financial instincts that had served him in London: land prices plummeted as the troubles in the country spread. But this did not worry him. Things had to improve, he thought. Meanwhile he was happy to be serving in his turn.

In about ten minutes he reached the top of the hill on the side of the park. His route had already curved so that he was in fact now on his way home. A few minutes' walk along the road would bring him to the shop where he collected his paper.

He noticed the sky was dark and smudged. Crows were flapping about. Down the road he could see the white dome of the temple near his shop. The flowers of the temple trees, frangipani, were out. White blossom. Those were the trees he would like to have on the borders of the land he bought for Siri. But the white of both the dome and the flowers was grubby, as though settled with ash.

Ray thought the sky should have cleared by now. He walked quickly towards the temple. By the wall he stopped to look again at the frangipani. Many of the white flowers had fallen. But in the garden next to the temple a tree with the blood-red variety of the flower stood in rich bloom. Ray was sweating.

Then, around the corner, he came to the shop: the charred remains of the shop. Bits were still smoking, thin wisps disappearing into the grey sky. A small crowd had gathered.

The vague thoughts in Ray's head evaporated; every muscle in his body was tense, but he felt extraordinarily calm. He stepped forward. 'How did this happen?'

Several people started talking. One man said the police had a statement from the JVP claiming responsibility. The shopkeeper was dead. He had been asleep inside. Kerosene had been used. Ray picked his way through the shattered glass and boiled sweets strewn along the roadside. Practically the whole of the tiny shop had been burned. One or two big blackened timbers still remained at the back, and buckled bits of the corrugated tin from the roof lay like petrified sheets of magma. The old *na* tree that had shaded the shop-front was scorched; the trunk looked as if it had been gouged with a hot knife. Two policemen had cordoned off the place.

Ray waited for a while absorbing the babble around him, watching the smoke rise in small puffs out of the heaps of ash. The veins in his arms were swollen. *A store burns like so many others up and down the country. Only this one's closer to home. Nothing else has changed.* But Ray knew that proximity made a difference. The air was pungent. He wondered whether the dust on his shoes now mixed earth with the ash of the shopkeeper's burnt flesh.

When he got home Siri was at the gate. 'Did you see . . . ?'

Ray nodded and brushed past him.

Siri had heard about the fire from a neighbour. 'Is it very bad?'

'The whole shop has gone. Completely burnt out.'

'Mister Ibrahim?'

'Dead. He was inside.'

Ray went to his usual place. The tea tray wasn't there. A fine layer of dust covered the table.

'Water's boiling, Sir. I'll bring the tea now.'

In a few minutes Siri came with the tea. 'Will you have it here on the veranda?'

'Inside may be better today.'

'You know Sir, they warned him. He was very foolish.'

Ray asked him who had warned the shopkeeper. Why?

'Several times they told him to stop selling those newspapers. Mister Ibrahim didn't listen. Even two days ago he told me that he will not stop selling newspapers just like that. But they said he must stop, or it will be the end for him. I don't know why he continued.'

Who had warned him?

'I don't know, Sir. These thugs who come around.'

Ray raised his eyes. 'Why do you think he didn't stop selling those papers?' he asked. 'He was not a Party man.'

Siri shrugged. 'He was a *mudalali*—a businessman. Making money. You make money by selling what people buy. People wanted his newspapers, so he sold them. That is his work. Was his work.'

Ray wondered whether Siri was right. Was Ibrahim killed by the market? Or was he simply caught in between? He could see the flames leap at Ibrahim's straw mat; within seconds he must have been wrapped in fire. But he must have screamed. How did they not hear it? The shop was not far, and the night had been so silent. The smell of kerosene? Flesh? But then, countries have been in flames before and the world not known.

'Sir, do you think there is any danger here?'

'What do you mean?'

'Will they harm this house?'

'This house means nothing. It has nothing to do with anyone.'

'I hope no harm will come. It is becoming so beautiful.'

Ray and Siri both felt uneasy all day. They avoided each other. Ray spent the morning alone and then went out to a café for lunch. He came back early in the evening and disappeared into his room. He had a shower and lay down on his bed to rest. Clean and cool; naked on the cotton sheet. He felt his body slowly relax. The evening was warm. As day began to turn to night the birds screamed again. Through his window he could see the sun set in an inflamed sky. When he closed his eyes the grey smudges came back. His skin was dry. He looked at the polished wood of his new windows. Siri had done a fine job. He had brought out the wood grain perfectly. Ray wanted to ask Siri to build another house. A house on *their* land out in the country. He thought if he provided the materials Siri could design and build a house with two wings, or even two small houses. One for each of them. If Siri were to marry it would make for a good start. Ray wondered how he'd feel if that happened. He would lose something. The intimacy that had yet to be. But he would feel some satisfaction. He would have made a difference.

Later, when he came out on to the veranda he found Siri sitting on the steps. Siri looked up; his hard black eyes gave nothing to Ray.

'Sir,' Siri said in a low voice, 'I want to go.'

'Where?'

'Away, Sir.' Siri remained sitting on the steps. His face was in shadow.

'What's wrong? What is it?'

'This destruction. I want to go away.' The eyes softened

slightly. 'And you, Sir, have seen the world. Tell me where. Where is a good place?'

Ray looked down at Siri. 'What do you mean? You know, shops have been burned many times before. In Matara, in Amparai, here in Colombo it has happened before.'

Siri shook his head.

'It has happened all over the world,' Ray said.

Siri kept shaking his head. 'But it can't always be like this. It can't.' The night air slowly curled around him.

'We have to learn. Somehow. We are no better, but we are no worse.' Ray turned on the wall lights, pushing at the darkness. Then he saw one of the new shutters was broken: several slats were splintered; the wood was raw. Ray felt a pain in his chest. He took a deep breath. 'Never mind. It can be fixed.' He was determined.

Siri stared up at him, then shook his head again as if at a fly. 'Sir . . . ' his face slowly crumpled. 'Sir, my brother back home. They've used a lamp-post for him.' Siri shut his eyes.

Ray's throat felt thick, clogged. 'You should have told me,' he said at last tugging at his neck. The body would have been mutilated, then strung up as a beacon; the corpse would swing in the wind for days. 'Why?'

Siri's bare feet dangled over the steps. When he spoke his voice was hardly audible. 'Who can tell, Sir, in this place?'

Ray looked at their shadows cupped in a circle of yellow light on the gravel below the veranda; the light on Siri's arms. He tried to lean forward but couldn't move. He couldn't clear the space between them. Siri's skin was mottled.

'It happened last night,' Siri said.

Ray nodded, 'Maybe you should take a few days off. Find your people,' he heard himself say. 'The veranda

can wait . . . ' His voice faltered. They were not the words
he wanted. Ray saw himself alone again in his house,
picking his way through the debris at the back. There
were two rooms still to be done; pots of yellow paint in
the corner of the bedroom would remain unopened. He
found himself thinking that without Siri he would have to
make his own morning tea again. Drink alone on his
incomplete veranda; wait.

But Siri said nothing. Ray could not tell whether he
had heard him. Siri slowly straightened out and stepped
down on to the path. He looked at Ray for a moment,
then turned and started walking towards the back of the
house, towards his room in the servant's quarters. Ray
opened his mouth to say something about the new
house, the cinnamon garden, but Siri had melted away
in the darkness. Ray remained standing on the veranda.
He felt he was on fire, but the palms of his hands were
wet. Out in the garden fireflies made circles. Frogs
croaked. The sky trembled like the skin of a drum.

CAPTIVES

SUNSET IS A good time to arrive in this part of the world, but I had expected them much earlier: tea-time was what the agent had said when the booking was first made.

Hearing the car turn in, I quickly dried myself. Nimal, my boy, would see them in, but I wanted to be there to welcome them: they were my first guests. While buttoning up my shirt I peeped out of my window. The man, a tall narrow Englishman, unfolded himself from the car. The dickey boot sprang open, and I heard the thump of baggage. Where the heck is that boy Nimal?

I would have been down straightaway but my zip got stuck and I had to pry the thing loose with a screwdriver. By then Nimal had turned up; I heard his squeaky voice. Somebody, I suppose Mr Horniman, rang the bell on the reception desk and Nimal called for me. 'Sir! Sir!' he shouted out, 'The party is here!'

When I got downstairs I found Mr Horniman leafing through the register. The lady, Mrs Horniman, had collapsed on the green armchair. She was staring at my flowers: lovely white lilies I had specially arranged for the visitors. Only then I saw how obscene the yellow stamens looked sticking out the way they did. But what's to be done? I hurried towards them and stuck my hand out.

'Good Evening, Good Evening!' I said.

They must have been driving all afternoon, down the hill road from Kandy through Matale and on. The lady looked exhausted, encrusted in a thin mud shell of sweat and dust. She had slipped her sandals off and was rubbing her ankle. Bits of red lacquer had chipped off her toe-nails. She needed a bath.

'Welcome. Please welcome. You must be Mr and Mrs Horniman. We were expecting you.'

Mr Horniman said they would like a good room.

I told him I had prepared the Blue Suite. 'It is perfect Sir,' I nodded in the lady's direction, 'for the honeymoons.' They were coming to me on the second week of their tour around the island; newly wed, I thought. Nimal picked up the suitcase with both hands and wobbled walking on the outer edges of his bare feet.

The Blue Suite is set apart in its own wing. There are two rooms and a bathroom. In the bedroom I have put a wonderful old four-poster bed with a lace canopy.

The lady was impressed. 'My goodness, this is the real thing.' The other room has cane furniture and opens on to a private patio. The garden beyond was deserted. The trees at the end of it were in shadow, and up in the sky Venus gleamed, nice and early.

I stepped into the bathroom and opened the sink taps. The pipes hissed and coughed and water spluttered out. I tested it. 'Look Madam, hot water!'

She was seated on the bed examining the bedspread. It was made of a special white lace. It came from up country, I was going to tell her. But I could see she was waiting for me to leave. She kept fiddling with her buttons, undoing the top ones on her blouse and making her bracelets go jingle-jangle.

I said there were many mosquitoes around and advised they kept the nets drawn across the windows. I switched on the fan and explained how the knob had to be turned backwards, anti-clockwise, because it had been installed upside down. 'But it works very well, Sir, no problem.' Then I also showed how the door to the patio and the garden opened. I asked if they would like some tea, but they said not for the moment. So I left them.

As I walked slowly back to my room upstairs I heard her laugh: a sound mounting over all the other sounds outside. How good it was to hear some happiness in this place.

When I first came there was nothing here. I mean it was a palace all right, a real *maligawa*, but a ruin not a hotel. I told my boss I would need at least six months to get the *maligawa* on the map. We were not far from Sigiriya and I believed, when the tourist trade picked up, there would be room for another hotel in the area. I was immediately appointed manager.

As it was getting dark I called Nimal and told him to light the brazier for the smoke and then make sure the corridor lights were on for our guests. We need to fumigate the place every evening. I have a special fumigation recipe from my grandmother who used to burn the leaves of the nutmeg tree, mixed with *dummula* resin, to keep away the insects at night. I found a nutmeg tree in the garden here when I came, and so every evening Nimal carries a smoking brazier of my special mix around the palace to ward off the insects. Fumigating.

'Now, Sir?' he asked.

'Of course now,' I said.

About ten minutes later I heard the hiss of the incense on hot coals. Nimal came rushing into the room carrying the small black pan, like a sorcerer's apprentice with smoke billowing out behind him. He did the front swiftly, tracing the perimeter of each room, before heading back towards the bedrooms. I heard him knock on the blue door. There was no immediate answer. He must have caught them at an awkward moment, but he stayed with the pan hissing like a cobra. Then I heard Mr Horniman call out and Nimal reply, 'Mosquito smoke.' He was let in; I thought for a moment that perhaps I should have taken the brazier myself.

After that I got the table set in the dining-room and went to check that the kitchen was ready to take the orders for dinner. I like to have everything planned and ready.

About an hour later I heard them come out of the bedroom. I was sitting at my desk in the lounge reading the newspaper. I have positioned the desk so that I can see all the main approaches to the centre of the *maligawa*. They came along the open walkway where I had the lights on for them. He held her by the arm and steered her, his head lowered next to hers, past the big olden-day moonstone I had set into the floor. I thought of the deer you sometimes see taking their first steps into a clearing, looking for food. The air out there was thick with insects and they ducked trying to avoid the flying ants and our huge moths that were banging against my pearl-glass lampshades; they hurried towards the lounge.

'Good evening,' I said, and ushered them in. Mrs Horniman wore a loose caftan which she drew closer to her. It was like a long large shirt and allowed the warm night air in right next to her bare skin.

They had both bathed and gave an impression of freshness, but I could tell from the way her shoulders drooped that she was tired. She had her hair plaited at the back and her face looked tender; the lips a little swollen. I found it difficult to take my eyes off her.

'We wondered about some dinner . . . ' Mr Horniman said.

I led them to the far end of the room and threw open the dining-room doors like a conjuror.

They both looked around the room. 'Is there no one else eating?'

'No, Madam,' I said. 'Tonight the whole *maligawa* is yours!' I seated them at the table. 'Now, something to drink first?'

Mr Horniman reached for his shoulder-bag. 'We have a bottle here, if that is OK?'

We do have beer, liquor, gin—everything, but guests are permitted to bring their own special drinks if they so wish. We have no wines, and no proper Scotch whisky yet.

'Do you perhaps have some soda then?'

I immediately snapped my fingers for my waiter. Jinadasa came with a white towel in his hands. He peered at me and I told him to bring glasses and soda. Meanwhile she touched a silver fork with her finger. Since they were our only guests I had asked Jinadasa to put our best cutlery out. That was done fine but he had used the heavy white china from our everyday set for the side-plates! Fortunately though he had got the napkins folded beautifully into lotus flowers.

While they were having their drinks I retired to the other room.

'Do you like it then?' I heard him ask as I left.

'The hotel's a bit empty but . . . '

'Not like the beach? Beruwela.'

I could see them on the beach. She would have a turquoise swimsuit. Her round throat dazzling as she turned her face up, away from the spray of the surf. The water would shatter like glass in the hot light. I wanted to say to them, you should see the east coast. Trinco.

Beautiful white sand, and you can walk for miles into the sea. But they couldn't go now, not with the war up there.

Then the damn lights went out. The whole place plunged into darkness. The cacophony outside increased tenfold: the shrieks of night birds, the roar of the jungle. I heard her call out timidly to her husband, 'Where are you?'

I made my way out to the back with my torch and shouted out for Nimal or Jinadasa. The bloody generator had conked out. Why did it have to happen this night, with our first guests here? There was a big commotion outside. Nimal was shouting. I told him to get the tool kit while I got an oil-lamp from the kitchen and took it in to the dining-room. I found them still seated at the table. I set the lamp down. It was smoking a bit but it made the skin of her hand glow against his arm.

'Sorry, sorry. I'm so sorry about this,' I said. 'The electricity has gone off. Some rascal has busted the generator. Excuse me. I'm very sorry.'

He told me not to worry. 'But will we have something to eat?'

'Oh yes, certainly,' I said. 'Electricity doesn't matter. Our *koki*, our cook, likes to use wood fire anyway. Anything you like.' I turned to her. 'Madam, dinner by candle-light. Like in Paris!'

'You have a menu?'

The menu was not yet available. 'Please say what you would like,' I said. 'Rice and curry? Soup? *Bistake*? Macaroni cheese?'

'What?'

'Sir?' Our *bistake* is very good. I took the initiative and recommended it. 'The *bistake* maybe? Actually it is *val ura* —wild pig. Very good. Some hunters brought it.' You have to take the initiative sometimes.

Mrs Horniman said 'Fine. Let's have that.'

'Very good, Madam,' I said, and melted back into the darkness. But I could hear them . . .

'Wild boar beefsteak?'

'It's wild pig, not quite the same thing.'

'Isn't it just the sow?'

She laughed. 'I think it's just the one of the litter that got away. *Lost* more than wild. A roaming piglet.'

They sounded quite cheerful; not put out by the adversities of the night. I suppose it is because they have each other, and therefore nothing to fear even here in the middle of nowhere. But I expected them to feel a little apprehensive: a big empty *maligawa* like this takes some getting used to. Outside I could hear the jungle flex and move. The jungle grass growing. Leaves unfurling. Things slithering around, searching, circling, fornicating. In between there was the terrible sound of metal on metal.

I went and gave the *bistake* order to *koki* and then went out to see how the repairs were going.

In that noisy darkness, with the oil-lamp flickering, Mr Horniman still looked calm. So far from home, waiting for food and for light, and yet seeming to understand that nothing could matter very much. The waiting didn't matter. There was nowhere to rush to. Nothing particular to do. Only to sit and pass the time. Only to sit and watch our tropical night shadows loom across his wife's face.

When the food was ready I sent Nimal in with the trolley. I put metal lids over the dishes: the grey steaks—*val ura* in coconut sauce—a plate of thickly sliced bread, fried bitter-gourd and sliced tomato and cucumber. The boy served them, carefully scooping out the sauce with a wooden spoon.

'Not bad, eh?' Mr Horniman said brightly.

Jinadasa got the generator going just as Mr Horniman was mopping up the last of his sauce with bread.

I went in to them as soon as the bulbs brightened. 'The lights are on,' I said.

'Very good,' Mr Horniman said. It was already nine-thirty. He looked at his wife. I could see she too was thinking of their bodies nestling in a bed of jungle moonlight.

'The *bistake* was good?' I asked. I wanted to know whether we were getting things right. It is best to know early so that you can rectify any shortcomings and keep your guests happy. I was most relieved when they complimented the food. I said I was very glad to be of service and offered them wood-apple for dessert. Then I asked them about the next day. Would they want to climb Sigiriya—the rock fortress?

Mr Horniman nodded firmly. 'Yes, tomorrow we want to see it.'

I said I would arrange everything. Nimal could take them in the morning.

'No, no, we can go on our own.'

'Sir, believe me it would be better for Nimal to guide you.'

'Isn't there a road straight from here, and then a path to the top?'

I wanted them to have a proper guide. I explained that Nimal would take them right to the top of the rock, and to the throne, and then bring them back in time for lunch.

Mrs Horniman interrupted to agree that the boy should lead them.

'But I wanted to explore. And why can't we do it alone? Always guides. You can't do anything in this country without guides.'

'Anything? Come on, don't be silly,' she laughed. 'Anyway I like that Nimal. He's sweet.'

Mr Horniman frowned, but eventually agreed. 'What

time should we go then?'

I suggested they have an early breakfast and set off by
seven in the morning. They would be back by eleven or
eleven-thirty then, before the midday sun.

'Is that long enough to see everything?'

'Sir,' I said in my gravest voice, 'you could spend your
whole life there and it won't be long enough. But for
tomorrow it is best to try and be back before midday. It
gets very hot in our country, you know.'

'But we want to see the frescoes and also the ruins.'

'No problem. You will see enough. Kassyapa, the king
who built the fortress, spent eighteen years there but,
you know, I think maybe he would have been happier
with a three-hour visit!'

'Kassyapa?' For the first time she looked at me as if I
had something really interesting to say. I felt my heart
quicken and tried hard not to let it show. I wanted to
impress her. To keep cool. The best thing to do was talk I
thought. Talk, talk, talk.

I asked whether she knew the story? How Kassyapa
built the fortress? Our famous lion-rock?

She shook her head, faintly amused I think by my
nervousness. I was so excited by her attention. I pressed
my tongue hard against my teeth until it hurt.

'We've heard about the frescoes.'

'But do you know what *he* was trying to do?' I asked.

They both shook their heads.

Films have been made about Sigiriya and dozens of
books written with all kinds of different theories. I have
seen none, and read none, but I told them what I thought
had happened.

Kassyapa was a prince whose father was a good sort of
man, but a fool. He was getting old and so he decided to
give his kingdom over to his proper son, Mogallana.
Kassyapa, who was a bastard—illegitimate—was going to

get nothing. But Kassyapa was an ambitious man with a lust for power and wealth. So he killed his father. They say he had him walled up alive in the mud of his famous water tank. At least according to the ancient chronicles. The brother fled to India swearing that he would one day avenge the killing and regain his rightful kingdom.

Kassyapa decided to make the rock Sigiriya his capital: an impenetrable fortress that would be the centre of the universe. He set out to be the god of his kingdom and planned Sigiriya as a pathway to heaven. Mount Kailasa, the ancient holy mountain, they say was created, or re-created, here.

They say that every bit of Sigiriya has been constructed according to this grand design to match it to the holy mountain. I can believe that. Without some such belief in what you are doing, how can anyone stay here in this wilderness?

When Kassyapa's brother came back from India with his enormous army, eighteen years later, Kassyapa came down from his citadel to fight on the plains. That's why he lost. Now, I ask myself: why did he come down to fight, if all his life he was building a fortress to protect himself? They say it was because he was so full of remorse he wanted to lose. Or that his evil deeds had so poisoned his mind that he couldn't think straight. But he couldn't have created the beauty of the place if he was so poisoned, could he? Could such a bad and wicked man create such beauty?'

'You mean the frescoes?' Mr Horniman asked. 'We've seen photographs. They are very beautiful.'

'I mean everything. In this God-forsaken place he created a real magic. The frescoes, the palace, the gardens. Could he have done all of that and still been the terrible man they say he was? A parricide?'

'But he was not the man who did it, was he? Not the

painter himself? He was only the king. Like kings everywhere.' She breathed deeply. Seeing her flesh suddenly move as she spoke startled me. Then she said, 'But you are right Mr Udaweera. History is not a simple matter.'

Mr Horniman looked at his watch. 'Perhaps you can tell us more about it after we've seen the place tomorrow. But it's late now, especially if we are to start at seven.'

I had kept them up much too long, but I felt they needed to know where they were, and where they were going. I bade them goodnight and watched them return to their room. To them it seemed my *maligawa* was just another night-stop—a steamy bed—in a passionate itinerary. But could they not feel something about this place?

I locked up my desk and did my late night stroll to make sure everything was in order before going to bed. Outside their door I stopped for a moment; then quickly walked on. I could see the sweat running down between their legs; stains like balloons ruining my brand new sheets.

Then a truck stopped on the main road. There were voices chanting, *raban* drums. I thought of my two guests, how they would have tensed up; holding each other, listening, imagining the worst: witchcraft, demons, bandits. The sound rose to a crescendo, then the truck moved on. The chanting and the drums receded. Ordinary jungle sounds returned to fill the night, but the intrusion lingered in the air.

The next morning I felt sluggish, puffed with sleep. My limbs ached. I suppose I had been worried about how things would go with them. I knew practically nothing about them and yet they seemed somehow indispensable to the hotel and to me. It was part of knowing that they had been there all night, partaking in the pleasures of a palace that was my *maligawa*, knowing that they relied on me for keeping them safe in their love-making, for ensuring their day went according to plan. Our destinies seemed intertwined.

After their two days at the *maligawa* they'd return to Colombo. Another week and they would be back in England. A garden with apple blossom and thyme and lavender. A kitchen with a fridge that didn't need mending. It was unreal. Across the lawn I saw Mr Horniman open the door and come out on to his patio. He yawned and stretched out, letting his maroon robe slip open. A tiny squirrel appeared on the ground in front of him. The black stripes on its back bunched as it crouched. It was nervous. Afraid of the big expanse it had suddenly found, the vast stretch of grass and gravel. Then suddenly it saw something and bounded off in a fast straight line.

Mr Horniman went in to wake his wife.

I could see her through the window on the bed with the white cotton sheet bunched under her. She looked up at him, uncoiling.

Then Nimal came across the lawn with a tea-tray tinkling in his outstretched arms. He put it down and knocked on the outside door. Mr Horniman came out on to the patio again. Nimal stood there looking at Mr Horniman—at his satin robe and the fair hair trapping the sun on his legs—as if he'd never seen anyone like him before.

'Goodbye, I'll call you when we are ready,' I heard Mr Horniman say eventually. Nimal waited a few minutes staring at the door chewing his lower lip. I decided then I should go with them too, up Sigiriya.

I met them after they had finished their breakfast and asked whether they had been comfortable. 'I hope the truck last night didn't worry you too much.'

They shook their heads. 'What was it?' she asked. She had a slightly dreamy look, as if she were thinking of something mysterious.

'Pilgrims,' I said. 'You get pilgrims going this way. They hire a truck or something for the village and travel through the night.'

'Did they stop here for rest?'

I explained that for some people the trance induced by these rituals is a kind of rest. It is time taken out of a hard and weary life. I wanted to support her.

'All that shouting!' Mr Horniman said, and got up to go.

When I suggested I would take them to the rock myself in my Jeep, Mr Horniman's narrow pointed head sank down. His mouth was tight. 'Sure, why not?' he said grimly. 'Bring the whole hotel.'

But she looked relieved, and asked whether I was sure I could spare the time.

I nodded happily and went to get the Jeep ready.

We drove right up to the foot of the rock and I parked under a tree. From there Nimal led the way, striking out in his grubby shorts, barefoot, with a stick in his hand. He used it to flick twigs and pebbles out of the way. Mr Horniman followed him like a slow giant—he was twice the boy's height. She walked a little bit behind watching the other two.

I caught up with her. The first part of the climb was gentle. Ahead of us Tikka chucked a stone at a green partridge sitting solemnly on a branch. He missed. Mr Horniman clicked his tongue like a father.

The lower reaches of the hill were wreathed in jungle scrub, clumps of dense undergrowth; and the earth was

41

pitted with small ravines. Above us the granite loomed.

'Are there animals here?' Mr Horniman asked fingering his camera.

Nimal looked up at him with a serious face. He was wide-eyed. 'Yes boss. Many animals. Monkeys, deer, tigers.' He gestured at the trees. 'Maybe in there, not easy to see. Dangerous at night-time. Elephants!'

Mr Horniman immediately searched the path for dung and footprints and checked the edge of the forest. But there was nothing. Only the tall dry grass, the thick bush and tangled trees. An army could hide there and he wouldn't know.

The hill gave way to a big black bone of a rock to which the earth, like flesh, clung in red strands. The stone sucked the heat out of the sky and radiated it back, stronger almost than the sun itself. I showed them the bathing ponds that had been built and explained the ingenious hydro-system, or at least what I understood of it. The two of them didn't say very much. They listened but seemed to be preoccupied with their own thoughts. I explained about the famous Mirror Wall they had seen from a distance. How it had stayed polished like a mirror for one thousand five hundred years. I told them about the graffiti etched on it through the ages, verses of lust and love for the women in the frescoes. And I told them to take care to be quiet because of the wasps in the big brown hives guarding the rock.

'Oh God!' she said fanning herself with a map. But when we came to the frescoes my two guests were completely overawed. Such delicate larger-than-life figures in the rock gazing out at the sky and the world and each other. Their golden skin almost turned the plaster into flesh. Long noses flaring out over large sensual lips. Pale amber eyes. Breasts heaving out of stone, the nipples lifting the thin transparent unbearable veils. Deep and perfect navels curving in.

I watched the other two take everything in inch by inch. Mr Horniman was peering through his view-finder trying to get it all in; he started shifting from side to side on a tiny ledge. 'What do you think?' I asked.

'Wonderful!' She touched my arm. I felt it burn. 'They are beautiful.'

Mr Horniman was clicking the apertures, whirring, snapping. 'Fucking shadows! If only the fucking sun moved.'

'So why did this king of yours have these painted here?' She stayed near me, ignoring her husband.

'I don't know. For his pleasure?'

She laughed and her laugh seemed to echo, perhaps just inside my head. Her fingers were wet. 'Here?'

'Some people say it was just the guards, an artist among the guards. But others say these are *apsaras*, divine angels. That hundreds were painted all over the rock face.'

Her windswept face pinched into a mouth of purple lips made her look more and more like an *apsara*: exquisitely alive. She ran a thick tongue over her lips rejuvenating them. I could feel her breath.

When he had finished photographing, Mr Horniman said, 'Should we go on?'

We climbed back down the open stairway to the start of the mirror wall. She let her fingers brush it, feeling the roughness of the words scratched in the plaster. We followed the bulge of the rock, sheltered by its overhang, and crossed an open walkway to the carved stone lion paws above. The carved claw alone was taller than Mr Horniman.

'It's huge,' she said.

I said that was why it was called the lion rock. Only the paws remained but originally the lion would have been colossal. Kassyapa's enemies would fear it from miles away.

From the paws it was a steep climb up the rock face through the lion to reach the summit. You had to scramble up footholds cut directly into the rock. Nimal and Mr Horniman started climbing, but she suddenly turned away.

'I think I'll stay here,' she said. 'You go on,' she told her husband.

I said I would stay with her, but my voice felt awkward when I spoke.

'Fine. Do that,' he said, and disappeared.

When we stepped back from the lion it felt as though the jungle unrolled like a carpet in front of us. The clearing, a small rust-red plateau, extended about fifty yards. At the edge was a cliff and then a drop of several hundred feet down to the plains below. Below us the jungle spread towards the ocean unfurling in a continuous green spray to meet the surf beyond the horizon. We were higher than anything else in sight except for the granite dome behind us. We sat in the shade of a tree and gazed out at the huge sky. There was no sound except for the wind. The babble of the jungle was flattened by the sun. Occasionally a hawk, or a kite, would flap its wings and stir the air.

She took off the thin cotton jacket she was wearing. It was hot, the air was hot and thick in my mouth; I wanted to say something to her.

'You will go back today?' I asked.

'Yes,' she replied. 'We have one more stop and then back to Colombo. On Friday we fly back.'

'To London?'

She turned and looked at me and nodded. 'Yes, another world.'

'You have a house in London?'

She said she lived in a flat, an apartment. 'It will be funny going back there, to be living alone again, after all this.'

I puzzled over what she said and then slowly realized that perhaps they were not husband and wife after all. 'This is not your honeymoon?'

She smiled at me. She didn't say anything. I wanted to ask her what they were doing here? How long had she known him? Did she have to go back? Everything inside me was racing. On that plateau alone with her I felt, for a moment, anything was possible. Kassyapa made this place his heaven. Surely that counts for something.

I looked down at her feet. She wore a pair of light blue canvas shoes. The thin material changed shape as she bunched her toes and the black and white ribbed elastic on either side of each shoe stretched in turn. She didn't have socks and her ankles and legs a third of the way up to her knees were bare. Her skin was a dusty gold. Her trousers which stopped short on her legs were tight round her calves. Each leg had a short slit at the bottom of the outside seam and a black button doing nothing. She was sitting with her legs apart, her elbows on her knees, cupping her face in her hands. She had undone her hair and it fell about her bare shoulders in wisps. It had curled into rings where it was wet from her sweat. I saw her arms were freckled. Small tufts of hair hung underneath in the triangles she made with her arms and her body. I could see the sky framed there, blue and warm.

I wanted her to understand that I was not a base or vulgar man. In my original plans for the *maligawa* I had included a large rectangular bathing pool made of stone, grey stone, with moss and lichen on its sides. The water would be like ink, dark with algae. I wanted big lily pads to hold the surface still, and pink lotuses sipping on top. I would have liked to have taken her there, to drink and feel the cool water, but we never built it. I wanted to touch her.

I wished I could remember how the pilgrim poets spoke their love. *The open lips, round cheeks . . . geese lifting their big wings . . . long still eyes and swans drunk with juice of heaven . . . fountains of flowers.*

Their lips once kissed warm flowers,
until flesh paint glazed them captive
in the chalk fingers of a king's rock.

Their long eyes now light a private court
impalpable as their rounded breasts,
while hot dry climbers make signs of love.

I want to but know I cannot match
the rhythm behind those curves, barely feel
the pulse that beats a lifetime at a time.

It is the rock I envy most of all,
that ruined rock that holds you
and still remains the bed of your being.

Could she imagine what I was talking about? I felt she might as well have been in the rock herself, and I a mendicant climbing a pointless stairway through a lion's wet loins, groping for hope.

When Mr Horniman appeared from between the lion's paws he looked hot and flushed but pleased for having done what he set out to do. He wiped his hands on his trousers as he walked towards us.

'You saw the top?' I asked, quickly. 'Nimal showed you?'

He nodded. 'Yes. Excellent.' He adjusted his camera strap. 'How are we doing for time? Are we late?'

I said no, his timing was perfect.

'Where's the boy?' she asked from behind me.

'He's coming, I was faster coming downhill.'

'You must be thirsty,' I said. 'In this heat you must drink. I brought some cool drinks in the Jeep.'

I got up and led the way back down the hill. I, like everyone else, left behind my confusions smeared on the walls of the rock. My legs felt damp.

When we got down to the Jeep I got Nimal to open the cream soda I had brought in the ice-box. Mr Horniman drank with great gusto, looking hard at me.

Then we clambered into the vehicle. The two of them squeezed into the back. 'Where's Nimal?' she asked.

'Don't you worry.'

Nimal jumped on to the trailer knob at the back and clung to the spare wheel. We bounced down the hill raising a cloud of red dust, scattering partridges off the road.

At the hotel I left them to their lunch and went and had a cold beer on my own at the back. The heat was stultifying. My head turned to stone. I slept in my chair for more than an hour and woke up only when Mr Horniman called out to tell me they were going. He wanted to settle up.

He took out a wad of notes and peeled off a number of them. He said, 'Keep the change.'

I didn't count the money.

She was already at the car looking towards the rock. I called out, 'Goodbye!' and a few seconds later they had gone completely out of sight.

I was staring at the place where the car had been when Nimal appeared with a bundle of soiled sheets in his hands. He lifted them up to show me. I told him we had to change them every day; that's what you do when you run a hotel. You have to.

47

BATIK

NALINI HEARD HIM go upstairs and close the bathroom door. She put a neatly wrapped chilled chicken down on the table and looked around the room. It was a small kitchen but there were cupboards on every wall; she thought they had done a good job refitting the place when they moved in a year ago. She and Tiru had planned the kitchen like professionals: calculating space for loading and unloading the fridge, washing lettuce, cutting meat, cooking, eating, cleaning up.

Tiru had discovered a talent for joinery and a real plasterer's hand. Nalini found she loved the smell of fresh paint. Together they quickly transformed the old terraced grey-brick London house into a home different from any other she had ever known.

Before them the house had been occupied by an elderly woman; she had died there, in her bed. The bed had been junked along with the rest of the furniture, but Nalini felt they had to peel layers off the whole place to get rid of the smell of old pee and boiled cabbage, and the stale bacon fat that seemed to grease every surface.

They hired a skip and threw out the carpets and the thick textured paper off the walls. Some of it came easily, already lifted by a black spotty mould, but in other places the paper was thick with generations of starched patterns. The old paper would bring huge chunks of crumbly grey plaster down, making big holes in the walls. Tiru would gently build a new layer suspended on a hidden lath and then bind it to the old plaster with a thin pink skim. There were polystyrene tiles on every ceiling which they patiently removed, chipping at grey limpets of cement with thin steel stripper's blades. They both wanted to be enveloped in a soft warm paint that would seep into the wood and the bare plaster.

Tiru and Nalini were in perfect agreement until it came to the through-room doors. Nalini wanted the doors in lilac. She had visions of the double doors between the sitting-room and the dining-room slowly opening and closing like two separate giant butterfly wings stirring the scent of honeysuckle into the air.

Tiru thought the doors were too big and that a dark colour would dominate the rooms, but she looked so disappointed that he gave in.

In the evenings when the lights were dimmed the lilac was deceptively delicate. She could make-believe she was in a Rajasthani palace: raw silk and bolster cushions, a crescent moon, a sky full of stars. But when the lights were turned up, or during the day when sunlight streamed in through the large bay window, it turned to a sorer shade of purple. Then the doors looked bruised and crooked. But Tiru never suggested they paint them again; it was only she who sometimes wanted to. Especially after last summer: she felt it might right a wrong or, at least, get them working together again.

In the beginning, even after hours of chipping at cement or Victorian hard-glaze, or cleaning walls with sugar-soap, or sanding down woodwork, they could scrape the dirt off their arms and lie together in a bath of almond oil soothing the cracks in their skin and still have the desire to discover new patterns in the warm contours of their bodies. The cast-iron bath was in a converted bathroom almost as large as their bedroom. They put ferns, a fig tree and a chair in it to fill the space and then lay there dreaming, their legs curled around each other in the water. Conches with their open pink lips lay by the chrome pipes. When they got out of the bath the steam would rise from their wet sloping backs and he would dry her with a large blue bath-towel, slowly running his hands over her, rubbing the towel right down to her feet, gently massaging, crouched on his heels. In the bedroom they had an old horse-hair mattress with a flannel cover. There she could touch his skin and feel the stream of his blood thicken; his body seemed solid, as if all sense of consciousness was forced up into the head. Her own head felt wrapped in a cloud: almost too airy. She told him how she felt she was in a permanent dream. *I can't wake up, I feel drunk.* Tiru would smile and say it was the turpentine and white plaster dust, the lack of oxygen in the room that made her feel that way. She would trace his lips with her fingers, his tongue, and hold his head in her hands.

Nalini looked back down at the chicken she had brought to the table. Her fingers were cold. She picked up a broad butcher's knife and split the plastic pack. Then with the bird spread-eagled on the chopping board she started to cut out the leg. Half-way through she bent it and snapped the bone out of its socket. She hacked at a bit connecting the leg to the thigh and pulled it by the yellow stump of its chopped off claw: the purplish flesh tore but did not separate and the rough, rubbery, goose-pimple skin slid and stretched until the quill-holes out of which the feathers had been plucked widened. She shook the bird and turned it over. She pushed aside the red cloth recipe book with her elbow and cleared the rest of the table. She felt she needed more room, or something. In the end she placed the knife edge on the bone and leaned on it with all her weight so it splintered. Bits of gritty red marrow crumbled. She then stuck her fingers into the crevice and twisted the meat until it came apart. Loose skin wrinkled up around the base revealing a grey knob of cartilage and little specks of white.

After she had got through the breast-bone of the bird she put the pieces in a bowl and rubbed in a paste of turmeric and yoghurt. It was Tiru's recipe. Then she washed her hands in the sink. While she was drying them Tiru came down quietly into the kitchen. He walked over to the fridge and got out a beer. He snapped off the ring-top and dropped it on a plate by the bread-bin. Then, without a word, he went out into the sitting-room. She heard him turn the TV on.

He had been like this for weeks. She would come home and find him buried in a newspaper or deep into television; he would acknowledge her with just a word or two and turn away. So she would go to the bedroom and curl up on the bed bunching her pillow into a ball between her arms and legs. She would squeeze it flattening her breasts and clutch herself. She wanted to stay there until he came looking for her. She wanted him to find her like that. She would wait staring at the walls they had painted together; the two small nineteenth-century Ceylon prints of fishing boats in Mannar, and the hills around Dimbulla, neatly framed and hanging next to the wardrobe. The thin pleats of the creamy rose curtains pouted where the hooks had become detached from the rail and the white nets behind them, against the windows, were discoloured. She could feel a kink growing under her ribs; sometimes she would bend and grip her knees but it wouldn't shift. She wanted things to be better than this.

When she had first told her mother about Tiru her mother had stroked her neck and said, 'Do whatever you think is right, darling. I trust you, but there are enough problems in life without asking for more.' She was Sinhalese, he was Tamil. Nalini was surprised that her mother thought such differences mattered. She was the one who told the story about an uncle who had fallen in love with a Tamil girl once; and how they had run away to Java because of the prejudices of the olden days. Nalini had been sure that they—she and Tiru—could show her mother the world had improved. Things come together, they grow better.

But Tiru never came up to her. Each evening she would wait and wait until her hope and anger evaporated in hunger and thirst. Eventually she would go downstairs and fix herself something to eat, then go and soak in a warm bath. When they spoke it was only to ask whether the front door was locked, or whether the rubbish had been put out; who'd let the milk go sour. Not like in the early days when she used to feel she knew what was going on inside him. Even when he was quiet she knew she was in his thoughts. Their lives were about themselves.

Before last summer he had only talked about Eelam— the call for an independent Tamil state—when they were with other people. He was not into politics; but people kept asking him about Jaffna. He used to laugh about it with her; he didn't know any more than anybody else about what was going on. Then in the summer they had both been stunned by the news about the killing of an army patrol up in the North and the murderous backlash against the Tamils in Colombo. The frenzied immolation of the island. The barbarity made the common memories Tiru and Nalini had found earlier of sesame oil and pink rose sherbet seem like so many sad and pathetic illusions.

In those first few days they felt helpless: too far away to do anything and yet implicated by every brutal act they heard about. The bright green tropical island they thought of as their own turned into grotesque images of smoke and devastation strewn across the news-stands, litter bins, subway walls and train stations of the whole city. Every time they met anyone the questions burst out: *What has happened? Why? Who's responsible?* And always someone would know someone who knew of something worse about yet another communal atrocity. Some claimed extremists had deliberately provoked the butchery to separate the communities; others said it was a carefully rehearsed plot by Sinhala chauvinists to burn Tamil families out house by house. But nothing could account for the mania that allowed the jeering and cheering for annihilation on the streets. In the world that Nalini and Tiru had brought together, the world they clasped so tightly together, they had thought there was no room for such things. They told each other how impossible it ought to be. Even so Nalini felt they were being prised apart by their past. Tiru had a sister married to a schoolmaster in Anuradhapura; they were both Tamil. Nalini had never met them; she knew no other Tamils still on the island. So while Tiru saw a real face crying, she felt she could only imagine one. The sister wrote and said they were trying to get to Canada where her husband had family they could join. Tiru sent them some money; Nalini prayed.

But as the months passed and the appalling news became almost routine, Nalini's sense of distress slowly gave way to a need to nurture her own strength. Her life, she told herself, was first to do with where she was rather than where she had come from. No one had a monopoly on brutality. But Tiru became completely caught up in the events back home. He would come back from work and switch from one news programme to another, going over and over the same images until the thin column of black smoke behind the reporter in Colombo drifted into every room in the house. He bought loads of newspapers and collected every article he could find about the troubles. He would spend hours with his red pen and the kitchen scissors cutting and marking, preserving the pain behind the stories. He seemed to want to brutalise his own sensibilities in an act of solidarity with the victims he began to call *his* people. He was getting embroiled in things he could do nothing about, and she could see it made him more and more despondent.

Then earlier this month Nalini had it confirmed that she was pregnant. She had always imagined it would be such a happy moment for them both, but Tiru was so distraught she dared not risk telling him. She thought he would despise her for so compounding their communal inheritances; it would be better to wait until things improved. Or bleed it.

She had tried to draw him out before. 'Why don't you talk to me any more?' she had asked.

Tiru had looked away. 'About what?'

'What you are thinking?'

'Nothing.' His face was impassive; his eyes were fixed on a spot near the ceiling.

Then this morning she decided there was no point in waiting any longer; she would tell him and hope he would remember the life they had once wanted. While he was dressing for work she asked him, 'Do you know what's happening?'

'What? In Jaffna, or here?'

'I'm pregnant.'

She thought his face lightened; she thought she heard him say *baby*, but then he frowned. His lips pulled in. He pushed a newspaper across to her. 'Now they are talking of bombing?'

'I'm *pregnant!*' she said again stretching the word and reaching to touch him, but he flinched and drew back.

Nalini heated some oil in a large pan and fried a handful of chopped onion. When the onion turned transparent she added the spices—coriander, cumin, cinnamon—and tipped the chicken in. She melted a stock cube in a cup of hot water and poured it in as well. Her hands moved mechanically. She brought everything to the boil and loosely covered the pan. The kitchen felt humid; the walls had a damp sheen on them and the windows had misted up. She went out, shutting the door behind her.

She peered into the sitting-room. Tiru was slumped on the floor against the double doors with his legs stretched straight out and a silent TV screen blazing.

'Do you want to eat? I am making some chicken.'

Tiru looked up in surprise. 'No,' he said, 'I am going out.'

'*Tonight?*'

Tiru looked away. The light from the television made his skin glow. His eyes were glassy. 'There's a meeting at the town hall.'

'I've made everything: chicken, rice, dhal . . .'

'It's a meeting about what's happening . . . in Ceylon.'

She could see he was anxious to go, she knew she should try to understand but tonight she had hoped things would be different; tonight she thought they might at last find something to celebrate. She felt panicky. She clung to the door and swung it, grasping at his last word.

'What do you mean Ceylon? Not Sri Lanka any more?'
She felt she was whining—*whining*—and stopped. He was
staring at her bare feet. She could feel them tingle, as if
the tufts of the carpet were alive. 'When will you be back?
We can eat then.'

'I don't know.' He looked at his watch. 'I'd better go.'

Nalini retreated into the kitchen. Suddenly the smell
of the chicken made her feel sick. She turned off the gas
under the pan and opened a window. She put her hand
to her mouth, holding her breath.

Tiru came to the kitchen and leaned lightly against the
doorway. 'You don't understand. I have to go,' he said
softly.

'No, you are the one who doesn't understand. You
think you know everything but you don't.' She picked up
the knife and scraped off the onion peel and chicken fat
into the sink. She wanted to cry. 'I feel sick!'

'What's wrong? Is it the baby?' Tiru stepped closer to
her.

'Everything. Can't you see?' She lifted the knife,
pressing hard against the sink. 'You don't even touch me
any more . . . '

'Have some water?' Tiru suggested quietly. He got a
bottle of carbonated spring water and twisted open the
cap; it hissed. He poured the water into a cup that was by
the bottle. The cup was decorated with a maroon pattern
and flecked with gold-leaf. 'Here,' he offered it to Nalini.
He held it in the palm of his hand.

She took it carefully from him, not letting her fingers
touch his. She didn't want him to hate her. She saw
nothing but the cup and his hand, an arm in a denim
sleeve. She lifted the cup to her lips; her fingers ached,
the water smelled of metal polish. She felt a thin hard
fork comb through her hair pricking her scalp and
coming down towards her spine pushing her belly out

more. She could feel him looking at her again. She knew he was standing there with his hands shoved back in his pockets; not moving. Suddenly she twisted from him and flung the cup away. She had never thrown anything so hard in her life. Although it took only a second to explode she could see the cup turn as it flew. The gold paint glinted sparking in the light and the water sprayed out in a wide slow arc splattering the floor and ceiling with silver drops: a chain of small pearls, tracer balls, needle markings trailing lines of dissolving perforations. Inside it was milk white, the bone stem curved up, cocked high, the rim finely modulated to a pair of pressed lips. When it hit the hard glazed wall the cup burst into a hundred tiny pieces of shrapnel. One larger piece, the crested base, dropped straight down and shattered on the green floor tiles. Water dripped down the wall making a puddle by the skirting board. Nalini's ears were ringing as if the air in the room had been decompressed. She watched the curved hulls of broken china rocking on the floor.

She crouched down; she could feel him fumbling, coming up behind her. She wanted to pick up all the pieces and stick them together with a lick of glue or spittle. She wanted to tell him that together they could somehow re-create it with a web of hairline cracks, like a real batik pattern. She felt a hand on her. It was warm. She knew he could feel her pulse. He pressed his hand to her and kept it there.

ULLSWATER

RANJIT SAID HE wants me to feel at home so he took me to a pub on the road above the lake. It was a fine summer's day. We sat outside. You must have some English beer, he said; he placed two pints of dark brown bitter between us and sat leaning forward with his elbows on the table. He had been wanting to talk to me ever since I arrived in England, but with his young family around there had never been quite the right moment until now. And now he was so anxious that his whole face became contorted when he spoke.

He said that lately he'd been feeling uncomfortable. He couldn't sleep at night. It was because of his father; he felt he knew so little about his father—my brother, Senaka—and he couldn't stop thinking about him. What the hell happened Uncle? He shook his head trying to clear it. What happened to him in the end?

I didn't know where to begin. I could hear sheep bleating in the field behind us. Up and down the long garden the borders brimmed with pink and blue English flowers: Senaka would have known all their names, but the foxgloves and hollyhocks out at the bottom of the garden framing Ullswater in purple are the only ones I know, and those only because I asked. It feels wholesome and safe, blessed, as if the air had been licked clean. I looked at Ranjit across the table. I wanted to tell him everything.

Two days before he died I visited your father, I began, back home. It was three o'clock in the afternoon. The sun boiled in the sky; the hot air rattled the pods roasting on the big flame trees by the road. Nothing else moved. Even the crows were stunned.

How can I forget it?

I banged on the gate, one of those wrought-iron affairs. The white paint was peeling; bits—round rusty shards— fell like blossom at my feet. Your temple flowers.

The house was run down. You could see the rain had destroyed the guttering on one side leaving the wall stained with big dark damp patches. The veranda looked a mess: chairs piled up at one end in the wash of some monsoon flood and boxes scattered all about. I even thought the house might be deserted, that Senaka—your father—might have gone away. Then a man appeared.

Where's the *mahathaya?* I asked.

Inside, he said.

I asked him to open the gate.

He took out a bunch of keys and unlocked the padlock. It was as big as a fist holding a fat iron chain; it slithered to the ground.

Call him, I said. Tell him Victor *aiya* has come.

The man disappeared inside the house. I waited on the porch steps. In the garden creepers throttled the blue jacaranda. Weeds had overrun what used to be flower beds and there were big bald patches under the breadfruit tree. The anthuriums had burst their pots and thick tongues of buffalo grass grew everywhere.

I hadn't seen Senaka for years, ever since I moved down south. There was never an occasion for us to get together. No reason to I suppose; we had our own worlds, our own preoccupations. He had his books, he was married, and in any case did not care for company, and I was busy running around trying to find a job, looking for ideas; I had tried all sorts of things before turning to teaching English: politics, newspapers, the post office, even the palm-oil trade—but for me it has always been a hand to mouth existence. Not like his. But then one day your mother, Sonia, wrote to say she had left him. She said he was not well but it was impossible for her to do anything for him. Apparently he wouldn't even look at her anymore. You were already studying in England and so Senaka was on his own. Things had gone very wrong for him and I felt I had to do something. I wanted to renew our frayed family ties. There was a lot of lost ground to retrieve. He was my brother and I had done nothing for him. It was not right.

I suppose I needed something too. The years—even then—already seemed to have just disappeared into nothing; I had frittered them away so foolishly. Now I have to take each day as it comes with liver salts and iodine and I know we have so little time however long we are given; and yet . . . We had each always been too proud of our independence. Even in our father's house, growing up, we quickly escaped in our own separate ways: he into his books, me into town. I never told him much about anything. He had to find out for himself like anyone else; he always seemed to know what he wanted to do anyway.

When we were children he was the one who always seemed to be examining the world bit by bit; searching, as it were, for something that would redeem it. Maybe it was because of our mother: she was so ill—so distant—although I think her problems really started only after his birth.

He was a great reader, your father; he read everything

he could lay his hands on. The second-hand bookshop on Junction Road near our house was heaven for him. Those days it ran a pay-as-you-read library service. You could buy a dozen books for a rupee and after reading them sell them back for fifty cents, or something, a week later. In this way most of England's literature passed through his hands. As he grew older the number of books he could afford to keep also grew and he began his own library, which he stacked up in precarious columns in his tiny room. From these books he learned about England in extraordinary detail. It became the country of his dreams: rich, fertile, full of a kind of tubby valour.

I was different, I was older than him: I was appalled at his infatuation with England. As an earnest young man I told him England was an occupying power that had to be repulsed. A blight on the spirit of freedom. In those days I was equally dismayed by our political leadership: at the time it seemed to me so uninspired. I wished we were in India where there was so much more of a struggle. Some fight, some idealism. Gandhi. Bose. You know, men who were doing something for their country. But Ceylon seemed full of lackeys. Everyone wanted to be Head Boy in the Governor's house. How could they? Only when the leftists started up in 'thirty-five did we begin to see a real future. They went out into the villages during the malaria to help our people. And the people recognized their concern. When the elections finally came they responded. I joined up.

But your father wouldn't dream of it. He was bright and could have done anything he wanted. He would have gone far in the system if he had wanted to. He could have joined the Civil Service, or done law, become a barrister, anything if he didn't want to fight for our natural rights. But instead in his mid-twenties he married your mother,

Sonia. It was a love match. One of the first in town. While he was meant to be preparing for his examinations Senaka, unnoticed, had gone courting. It surprised everyone. We knew her as the daughter of a very wealthy fellow who lived on the other side of town and the marriage was seen as quite a coup. Everybody talked about it.

People even said he had used a magic spell—a *mantram*—and so on, but I don't think Senaka himself knew how he did it; or why.

I remember your mother as a slim elegantly dressed girl with a big open face. It was flat as a plate and extraordinarily pale. In the evenings, in the afterglow of sunset, when parrots darted across the sky, her face would absorb light and slowly become luminous like the moon. She was a lovely girl in those days.

Quite frankly I don't really know what she saw in him, but then I can't say I understand how these things happen. I could never let go of myself like that; I always thought you should find yourself first before you embraced someone else, a stranger.

But it was all very sweet. He used to take strings of marigolds for her wrist: velvety, bittersweet flesh flowers. One time I saw them—the flowers—trailing down his leg and asked him where he was going. He said he was going to the bookshop. With marigolds? I asked. He quickly stuffed them into his pocket. I want to look something up, he said. Botany. His face flushed.

The wedding took place within the year. I suppose it gave our parents some joy in those last years of their lives, although it was hard to tell with mother being the way she was.

Your grandfather, Sonia's father, said at the wedding, in front of us all: My daughter must have the best. I'll give you a house, a good start, but if you ever make her unhappy—he cocked a fat yellow finger at Senaka—I'll put a bullet in you myself, understand? And he might easily have done if he had lived long enough. He was an ox of a man. In the beginning the house seemed such a blessing to Senaka. I always thought it was one of the loveliest in town: large and rambling with that stone floor polished like marble and the ornate carved wood frieze—the *mal lella*—under the roof, the Dutch tiles. It was so much more gracious than our cramped bungalow. Your father was so proud of it. He showed me how he had turned one of the bedrooms into a study and lined the walls with his books. You remember how his window opened to your garden full of such grand old trees: mango, king-coconut, bread-fruit.

Marriage protected your father from my needling and allowed him to indulge completely in his quaint English manners. Love, he knew from his reading, was not only blind but blinding. Desire blinded. It gave him the privilege of wallowing in his fantasies. While I measured each day's news against our goal of self-government he compared new verse, fresh as apples from England, to the Lake Poets he'd committed to memory. And he managed to feel the more virtuous of us. He seemed to grow older much faster than I did.

Then came the war: in those days the talk in town was all about the Japanese air-raid and the Soulbury Commission, the jailing of the *Sama Samajists* and the struggle for our national independence. Fighting talk. For me it was heady stuff, but when he and I met it was as if nothing were happening in the world. Even when they dropped the atom bomb he said nothing. Somehow by then his incredible dismissal of the daily news—the exigencies of our lives—had a strange authority over anything I could say. He was able to engender such inhibitions in me that it became impossible for me to talk to him about anything serious without feeling I was babbling like a little boy. He, rather than our poor unfortunate parents, had come to represent family stability and authority.

By tacit agreement we also never talked about his marriage, even though the wedding had divided our world, his from mine. And so, slowly, we drifted apart and that common memory of childhood which was once practically the whole of our lives—picking *jambu*, escaping to the tree-house, tense cricket matches played by ourselves—shrank and became a tiny core wearing itself out. Our words to ourselves outnumbered everything else in our heads. Whenever we met, in those early years, your mother would leave us alone to talk but we would just sit on those wicker chairs on the veranda and speak about the baker's bloody bread, or some technical problem with your father's gramophone . . . Then one of us would get up abruptly and say, Must go now, and that was that.

He became such a conservative—that was the thing. It was as if, having found your mother, nothing else mattered to him. While people like me ran around vainly trying to shape a new society, he preferred to sit in his garden and watch his flowers grow, or read his books of faraway places in the light of a yellow desk lamp and dream of another world. I really couldn't understand it at the time.

Then you were born, and he discovered how little he had that was his own. He complained to your mother that not only was the house not really his own but everything in it seemed to belong, in its origin, to somebody else. The tables, the cupboards, the china, the crockery, even the bed they slept in had somebody else's imprint on it. Everything was a gift, and every giver had purchased a small claim on his life, a claim on his well-being. And

everything came from your mother's side; from her
father, or mother, or an uncle, or an aunt. Even you—his
baby son—had your mother's features, her family
bounce. As a child you had nothing of Senaka as far as he
could tell; not even that slight tilt of the head that had
kept our people listing but afloat generation after
generation. And the mandarin comfort of his home
which he had taken such care to protect from the harsh
realities outside suddenly appeared to him to be a
complete illusion. Nothing had been protected. The
whole island had a finger in his life, while he himself had
nothing. It soured him.

Your mother had been his only link to the rest of the
world; she dealt with all the practicalities and fed him
the bits he needed to nourish his life. She must also have
given him some real warmth. But after you were born I
think he felt she was slowly leaving him stranded inside
his tight, tight head.

In those days up in our hill country the stars at night
were so close you could almost touch them. They
swarmed across the sky like a million tiny mirrors of our
earth. I used to feel proud just seeing them—as if they
too were somehow ours—but Senaka found no solace.
He felt that the stars had all turned against him. I think
to him it was as if the whole place, the times, the land,
the sky, the country, family, history, destiny all conspired
against him. After our parents passed away he just
withdrew. Your mother told me he had become closed
completely, hunched up. She said that when their eyes
met it was no different from meeting the gaze of a stray
cat. That was when, as you remember, he retreated to his
study and stayed with the door shut. In his bit of territory
at least I guess he felt safe from the twists of the world
outside; comfortable with the sound of a heavy ceiling
fan swishing the air, the muffled thud of books closing,

pages decaying, himself growing old. Outside there were the crickets, the cawing of crows, and occasionally the crash of an overripe bread-fruit falling through the thick leaves of that huge tree.

Anyway, when he finally appeared on the veranda that hot afternoon in 1967 when I went to his house, his eyes were screwed up against the light. His mouth was lopsided. He wore a banyan over a crumpled sarong and scratched at his head as he walked.

Were you sleeping? I asked. His face was rubbery. He nodded and sat down on one of his wicker chairs. He took a deep breath but said nothing. I could smell arrack coming off his skin: an almost visible vapour fermenting the hot afternoon air. The place reeked of liquor.

He expressed no surprise at my suddenly turning up after so many years.

How are things? I asked. Are you OK?

He shrugged. I don't know, he said. Are you? His eyes were briefly defiant. He spoke with his chin to his chest, his eyes fastened on his knees, but every now and again they'd flick up to check who might still be around. He rubbed his forehead as he spoke and his face glistened with sweat. He was unshaven. Tiny beads formed like warm dew on his peppery upper lip.

I asked about your mother.

She's gone away, he replied quickly. He didn't say any more as if he wanted to forget some misunderstanding.

So we just sat there breathing in each other's air. A couple of flies settled on the table.

It wasn't the first time we had sat like that in silence. Only this time Senaka looked about to burst like the dusty pot plants in the garden. His bare feet were swollen. He had always looked serious as a boy. His brows, nose and mouth used to rush together to the centre of his face, pulling it into a permanent frown. Now they were puffed

71

up in different shapes, distending and distorting his face into something soft and vacant.

What's happened, Senaka? I asked. I wanted to capture some of the time we'd lost. Life was passing by too fast I wanted to say. Too fast for us to sit there saying nothing.

He lifted his head and looked at me suspiciously. I'm all right, he said. What do you think?

The veranda with the dark grand lounge behind it had such a mysterious air. You must have felt it too. It was a front: a place for small talk, entertainment. It was the foyer of a theatre which then became the theatre itself; a stage for lies, artifice, pretence. Neither of us had the stomach for it any more.

Your father stood up and said he had a headache; then, bowing his head as if in a plea for clemency, he suggested we go to his room. The arrack on his breath was sour. He headed towards the back of the house, walking close to the wall, steadying himself every now and then by testing it with the heel of his palm. His head was cocked at an angle. He swayed a little and left a trail of cheap coconut liquor in the warm air. I followed him.

When he opened the door to his study I felt we had walked into a lair. Nicotine clung to everything, the wolfy stink of gut-rot: diarrhoea and stale smoke. He had a lavatory adjoining his room; it had no door. Old screws on the frame had rusted and released a brown stain down the sides. The small square sink was cracked; a dead cockroach lay on the edge by the bits of dry green soap. His roll of toilet paper had unwound from a wooden peg and there were rags plugging a leaky cistern. I could see him sitting on the commode every night with his head in his hands, retching, spluttering, drinking his ropey arrack from a bottle on the wet floor, bleaching out his stomach; too drunk to unhitch his sarong when he finished.

There was a tall glass with a finger of yellow liquor already on the table. A cigarette lay burnt-out on the arm of a chair with two inches of ash curling like a grey horn.

He opened a cupboard and picked up another glass and a half empty bottle. Arrack? He showed me the bottle.

I said, Fine. I wanted to make some gesture of good will. I was willing—God knows I was willing then—even though I felt sick inside. I looked around the room. In a corner on a table was the old gramophone with a broken lid, and two cane armchairs—*hansi-putu*—and a sofa-bed by the windows.

Senaka put some ice in the glass from a small fridge he had installed in the room and sloshed the liquor in: the ice cracked like a pistol shot. He then filled his own glass. We sat on the armchairs. He closed his eyes and said, Cheers! His voice was already thickening. He didn't look at me.

For a long time we just sipped our drinks while I tried hard to think of a way of bringing us back to life. It was so hot and wasting. We just sat there like strangers. I said nothing. I couldn't help it.

Then slowly he started talking, the words coming faster and louder as he spoke; in a harsh bitter voice he started accusing me. You always thought I was bloody useless, didn't you? he said. A lackey. A sponge. The monkey in your glory parade . . . His eyes were half closed, the skin around them twitched. You hated me. You hated me for intruding, for being born, for being me. For not being one of you. You thought it was all my bloody fault . . .

I felt poison burning my lungs. Each word was wrung out of his mouth with such bitterness. Hate?

I told myself he was not well. I told him, It's all right. Take it easy. But then he shouted at me.

I said OK, all right. I lifted both my hands, open and

empty. I surrender. I give in. What do you want? I asked.

Don't fucking patronize me. I want nothing, he shouted. I've got what I want. What the hell do you want? Why did you come?

Then he started shouting about mother. *Our* mother. As if he thought I blamed him for her illness. Maybe I did once but that was so far back, I had put it behind me. I wanted to reach him again so much. I came to help— what are we if we can't help each other?—but anger was climbing up inside my throat. He had no right to shout at me like that, to talk like that. I felt all wired up inside.

There is nothing left, he then said quietly. We are on our own, until we are dead we are on our own. You can't get away from that. He dug one hand into the other.

What about your son? I asked. About you. I thought he must recognize some responsibility.

But he looked at me as if he didn't know what I was talking about. He then crossed his arms tight against his chest and closed his eyes. Just get out will you, he said. Go! Leave me alone. His eyes were squeezed tight. I don't need you here. Get the fucking hell out of here, he shouted again.

I wanted to smash the glass in my fist, hammer some sense into him, but I controlled myself and very carefully put the glass down on the table. My hand was shaking. My shoulders felt swollen and the blood throbbed at the back of my head. I felt all hot again; the sweat broke out of my skin and soaked the back of my shirt. It dribbled all down my spine. Almost every single moment of frustration, every disagreement we had ever had, every argument from the most trivial over a cricket ball to the most profound over democracy voiced and unvoiced returned like a flood to fill me with all the fury I had ever felt about him. But I held it in; my whole body began to go numb.

I was so angry with him for making it so. For his drunkenness. For his hopelessness. I could not bear to stay a minute longer. There was nothing I could do that I wouldn't later regret. I got up to go.

Then he opened his eyes for a moment and I saw something drop behind them. Just for a moment he looked vulnerable and weak—so frightened—but it quickly faded. It was too late. I walked out. I went as fast as I could with that frightened angry look on his face clinging to me; it stuck inside and has stayed stuck.

Two days later he was dead. He shot himself in the head.

I still feel cold to think about it . . .

When you came back from England for the funeral no one wanted to say anything; there seemed to be no need. The coroner was kind and you had to get back for your finals.

Then later when you got married here in England and settled down I never expected to see you again. I knew there was nothing for you back home after what had happened: only me. Your mother told me how you had said you never wanted to see her again after she remarried. I felt like writing to you then. It was not her fault. There was nothing else she could have done; she couldn't have coped alone in that house. But I didn't write. I don't know why. I suppose I was waiting for something . . .

So when you wrote inviting me to come and meet the family, and arranged for the ticket and all, I was really happy. I thought maybe there was some hope then, at least for you. You know, among my papers I had come across a big brown scrapbook full of cuttings collected by your father. The pages were brittle, riddled with holes; the edges crumbled into yellow dust in my fingers. It had all turned into so much rubbish, good for nothing but silverfish and weevils: everything had felt so pointless.

I had been staring out at the black water while talking. When I looked back at Ranjit I saw he was about to cry; his face was lopsided, the skin tugged down by his mouth.

But what did my father really want? he asked. What the hell did he think he was doing? . . . Ranjit's voice was so harsh.

Surely he understood his father had turned into a drunk, that he had become ill, and that he had deliberately cut himself off? But Ranjit seemed to want me to exonerate him. Us.

In the end I said, Your father knew what he was doing. In his own way he *knew*. There wasn't anything more I could say.

I sipped the beer, Ranjit's English bitter, and waited for my mouth to go numb.

STORM PETREL

I WAS GOING up Woburn Walk to a second-hand bookshop when I bumped into CK coming out of a travel agency. CK was a small thin man in his late forties; he wore a brown tweed jacket with a bright red woollen tie. He was startled, but then we recognized each other.

'How are you?' he asked quickly, looking rather pleased.

I mumbled something.

'I have been back home, to Sri Lanka!' His winter skin had been warmed, the brown was deep; he looked healthy.

'Oh yes.' I nodded.

'Yes! Yes!' he said excitedly, 'Just before the hot weather. Wonderful. When . . .' he pushed back the spectacles sliding down his nose, 'when did you last go back? To Sri Lanka?' Now he was beaming.

I had to think hard. I am useless at measuring time. 'About four years,' I guessed.

'I went about then also. 'Seventy-nine. How different! You can't imagine. Then ten rupees, even five rupees, was good money. You had something you know. But now! Everybody has fists of money. Fifty rupees, hundred rupees, it's just nothing. Nothing!' He shook his head in amazement but did not elaborate on whether this was inflation or prosperity, whether he approved or disapproved.

His sense of amazement was infectious. The grim wet May air suddenly cleared and the midday sun flooded the little alley we were in. The air lost its chill and the warm buds and curled green leaves of the plants in the pavement tubs seemed to open before us.

CK carried on like one of those indefatigable South Asian steam engines. 'East Coast, West Coast, North, I went everywhere. I also went to India you know. The South. Madras, Trivandrum, Goa, you know Goa? Cochin. All nice. Goa and Cochin especially. But Ceylon . . . ' he took a deep breath and tightly crumpled his mouth so that what was his smile hovered only in his eyes. He slowly shook his head. 'Ceylon is now very prosperous. You know they are building houses all over the place. And very modern too. And tourists all over. All over the place. East Coast, West Coast, all over. You can't go a hundred yards—tourists! India is even more full of them,' he added, in case I planned to offer a comparison. 'In India young people, not hippies and all, but just young people are roaming all over. All kinds of young people, boys and girls sleeping anywhere. You won't believe how happy they are! I asked them, you know, What are you doing? Do you like this sort of wandering?' His voice pitched high, rising uphill. 'But you know it's very good. They love it! They come from Norway, Sweden, Germany, and they don't want to go back. It is really amazing. They sleep on the street or station and can eat for two rupees. What more is there in life, huh? They are looking for *dharma*. I also slept in a station in India.' CK cocked his head and smiled, almost forgetting me in his contemplation of that hot night in a southern station, sharing a platform with a bevy of sweaty moon-eyed wanderers.

I was impressed. CK was so enthusiastic, and seemed to have travelled with such wonderful curiosity, talking to everyone about their lives, their hopes and their migrant dreams. *And are you happy?* I could so easily imagine him interviewing them with his large open smile creasing an already quite wrinkled narrow face. I could see him peering forward and asking earnestly for the *really true* answers. Their responses he would settle in his head by patting his grey temples very gently.

'You know I'm going back,' he said, as if clinching some complex argument. I did not react. I was not altogether there with him. I was in India. He repeated his statement, 'I am going back—home to Sri Lanka!'

'You mean for good?' I asked, catching up.

He sighed longingly, 'Yes soon. I just now was inquiring about tickets!' He nodded at the travel agency.

'I went on this last trip really to view things you know: the prospects. That is why I went to India as well. People say it is picking up there also. But back home is even better, now.' He looked over my shoulder into the distance at the many possibilities: London, Madras, Batticaloa. 'I have more or less made up my mind. You know what I will do? I will go to the East Coast and open a little guest house there.' This must have been a thought that had occurred, or even a decision made, minutes before our encounter but which had quickly assumed the appearance of a lifelong dream. It must have been what caused that wonderful exuberance which filled the air when he first spoke. But the full potential of his happy vision seemed to hit him only as he continued. 'Yes, you know what I mean?' He looked appealingly. Then, almost in a dream, he said, 'Just a little place. A sort of *guest house.*' The last two words were worked around his mouth to savour every last drop of magic in them. Already he had a proprietorial air about him basking in London's spring noon.

A rich spice smell drifted from the samosa counter a

few yards away to add to our exotic shared vision of CK on the East Coast.

'Are you going to build it? Like a hotel?' I asked.

CK looked surprised. Then with a benign smile he explained 'No, no. Not a hotel, but a simple guest house you know.'

I felt sheepish. Of course not a hotel. A hotel in Sri Lanka has hundreds of rooms, swimming pools and cocktail bars. It has concrete; waiters in crisp white sarongs; Sunday curry buffets; conspicuous Bar-B-Q dances; three-day-island-tours; Serendip gem stores; batik dresses and shy girls employed for their simple faces and bare midriffs. Hotels are built by international conglomerates, not individuals you meet on the street.

'Actually maybe *cabanas* would be better. That's what these tourists like nowadays. You know what I mean?'

I said I did, but he insisted on clarifying the meaning.

'You see, it is really just a cabin. Very simple. I will have it like a hut. Some cement, and you know our coconut thatch? *Cadjan.* I will put that. Costs very, very little. And the less it has nowadays, the more these tourists like it. They pay more in fact for less!' He beamed again. 'So I will just have a few of those. That is all.'

He was already there, sitting on the veranda of his own modern bungalow enjoying a panoramic view of the Indian Ocean and his plot of *cadjan cabanas*. I too gazed longingly at the mile-long line of white surf rolling on CK's beach.

Then he had another idea.

'You know there is no problem about food. Always there is a *kadé* nearby where you can get rice and curry for a few rupees. And these tourists, they like that.'

'Ah good,' I said, 'I was wondering about the food.'

I was thinking to myself that it would be worth opening a restaurant near CK's beach. It would be a better idea than the *cabanas;* you could live without a thatched hut but you wouldn't last long, even in paradise, without food.

'I also went to the small towns, you know.' CK lifted his eyebrows and with the same action lifted his whole scalp. 'It has changed so much. There's no denying, it has certainly changed. We have developed a lot you know. You should see the houses there now.'

He was so persuasive I wanted to return immediately with him.

'The houses are just like in Colombo now, much better than in this place.' His face became very serious, his mouth purposefully turned down at both ends. 'You know what the reason is? Everybody now has somebody in the Middle East. Working there. Earning pots of money. Then they get everything. You know, TVs—televisions—cassettes, videos, motorcycles, the works! And still the *kadé* is there with our *thosai* and sweet tea. Unbelievable, no? But . . . ' CK then smiled again as if he was passing over a secret, 'in some ways nothing has changed. You know what I mean?'

I knew what he meant. It reminded me of the happy times when, as a child, I would smuggle home spicy sweet packets: mixes of cardamom, gram, almonds, saffron and silver coated sugar pearls. A deep impossibly personal pleasure.

'You know the real things are still there. That is why I have decided to go. Have you been to the East Coast? You know beyond the lagoon and all: Nilaveli, Kuchchaveli. Around there is where I'm thinking of. Good sea, white sand. And very warm.'

We were both silent for a while. The salt in the sea air lulled us almost to a sleep. Overhead the sea breeze echoed the roar of the surf as coconut trees brushed their heads together, whispering like giants planning our destiny. The sun was hot. CK was going over each step of his dream. But in just two months the whole island would be engulfed in flames: the East Coast like the North would become a blazing battleground. Mined and strafed and bombed and pulverized, CK's beach, the dry-zone scrub land—disputed mother earth—would be dug up, exploded and exhumed. The carnage in Colombo, massacres in Vavuniya, the battle of Elephant Pass were all to come. But that day in the middle of London in the middle of May we knew none of that.

Eventually I asked CK about his schedule, 'So when exactly are you going back?'

This innocent question stopped his whole happy train of thought. Suddenly he was thrown back from the Land Registry office in Trincomalee to our sunny walkway in Bloomsbury. But the wheels soon turned smoothly again.

'I am thinking of going back in about six months time. I have a few things to settle, then I think the time will be right for me to go. You see you can't rush these things. You know how it is, going home. But definitely by next year I think I will be there.' He looked at me as if for confirmation.

Involuntarily I nodded my approval. I could see he was pleased. The plan was falling into place under a logic of its own; there was a kind of effortless imagination at work. He said he felt he was a lucky man. For ten years his imagination had soured slipping on the spinning rungs of the clerical grades in his Euston office. His expectations, even his dreams, had learned to conform to a fixed and finite set of small increments. Now, suddenly, he felt he had a new dimension—a free future —to explore. He seemed twenty years younger in a world of his own making. He looked at me and said, 'You know, I am already a happy man now.'

Then the sun slipped behind a cloud and shadows

rushed the ground; we both became aware that it was late. Our lunch plans had become distorted. We nodded vigorously to each other and parted company. CK craned his thin neck like a bird searching for the sea while I hurried on to my bookshop.

Ranvali

I LEFT AT the crack of dawn. My father had loved driving out at first light to see day gently break on the road, the grey turn silver between the coconut palms and the countryside slowly come to life; his would be the only car on the road: a gleaming mulberry bonnet heading south, the slim whitish trunks of the palm trees flashing by and the yeasty blue blur of the sea foaming; going like the wind. Inside, my speeding heart sang; the cool sea and the last trace of night slipped over my arm trailing out of the window; towns, roadside stalls, bullock carts, cyclists, *tirikkeles*, whirled past in a wake, lost to sight and forgettable. I was driving down to Ranvali, father's beach bungalow, to find out what it was like now; I hadn't been for so many years.

The bungalow is down a bumpy lane off the main coast road. On one side of the lane there was a long tall hedge of red hibiscus flowers with buds tightly rolled into bundles. On the other side huge plantain leaves like tattered temple flags hung over the road, browning at the edges. The old bungalow itself looked shabby. My uncle keeps an eye on the place and Carolis, the caretaker, probably looks after it like his own, but it needed a fresh coat of paint and some new cane tats. It looked smaller than I remembered: a little bungalow on a thin spit of land sticking out into the sea. The pounding of the ocean was everywhere.

When the car rolled into the driveway the place felt so familiar. The wind coming from nowhere, above, rushing inland; opening the door and feeling safe in a pool of warm still air below the turbulence. White butterflies rose up from under the door and bobbed about before settling down again to feed on the dung a few yards away. Beyond them a hen pecked its way around the shaggy base of a coconut tree. There were patches of intense sunlight burning white holes in the ground. The same holes as always.

But then Carolis appeared. His face was a web of deep cross-hatched lines and his small eyes were cloudy. His moustache had turned white as if bleached by the sun; it looked unreal. He was much thinner and frailer than I had expected.

Seeing him released a flood of memories: the afternoons I'd spend gathering baby coconuts from our seaside garden while father snored outdoors in a long uninterruptible siesta—beautiful miniature husks the size of my hand, fresh green and smooth with rich brown caps of petals that peeled off in clingy rubber flaps; warm brown eggs, guava jelly; sweeping sand castles with long thin *ekels*—the dry spines of palm fronds; looking for bee-eaters and kingfishers and humming-birds; making paper boats with Carolis, watching him square the paper, fold it, run a shrivelled yellow thumb-nail down to sharpen the crease, a turn here, a bend over, Look Jo-*baba*—magic! He had big crooked teeth in those days and his face was much bigger. We would go to the lagoon where I'd launch my boats with little messages stuck into the folded centre cone. I imagined them catching one of those ocean currents I was always being warned against and

or even Russia, where someone on a
vould find my note and read all about me
arolis rocked back on his haunches and
xcitement while I pushed the water to
go out further. But now his face was so
sunken it seemed as though he hadn't laughed in years.

I asked him how he was. He nodded at me; a betel-
stained almost toothless grin slowly split his face. 'Good,
Missy,' he said, meaning life goes on. His boy unloaded
the parcels from the car.

'There is some *thora-malu*—seer-fish for lunch,' I said.

Carolis nodded some more. He was small and stooped
and dug out. Practically his whole life had been tied to
Ranvali. Father had brought him to the bungalow before
I was born and he had stayed on.

He called out for his boy to bring some *thambili*—king-
coconut—to drink. The young boy came with a bunch of
puffy yellow nuts, each bigger than his head. He looked
at me very shyly and then crouched down to separate the
biggest one from the rest. He spun it around expertly in
one small hand slicing oval palettes of the husk with a
long curved knife until there was only a thin white tight
flat membrane on top. Finally, using the beak of the
knife in a grand flourish, he chopped a square hole for
the water to flow through.

I asked Carolis about the village and the disturbances
in the area, but he didn't seem to want to talk much. I
was not the little girl he knew. He took me around the
bungalow; the place was spartan inside, scrupulously
clean. It had been sprinkled with disinfectant. He was
watching me for my reactions, but I felt too awkward to
say anything. Eventually he said he would go and prepare
lunch. I went for a walk on my own past the lime grove at
the side of the bungalow and up the hill. At the top, on
the dry crab-grass, I let the warm sea-air blow over me.

My hair was already thick with salt. It felt tough and woody like coir. From the hill you could see the ocean—the Indian Ocean—turn into the lagoon and churn the water with blue sea-suds. Yellow flowers and spindly coconut trees leaned towards the sea, where the white surf curled on a ribbon of slowly disappearing gold sand. Ranvali was the last bungalow on that slip of land: a square of red tiles and a neat fenced garden. I wished I had come sooner.

Carolis had set a table on the front veranda with a batik table-cloth, a blue tie-dye, with a sunburst in the centre. The ends were weighted down with small stones to stop it from blowing off in the wind.There was grit in the rice Carolis served. I had to pan each mouthful with my tongue. 'It is impossible to get a decent measure of rice these days,' Carolis said. Later, when the sun was down a bit we walked to the sea.

As we walked Carolis began to talk about father. He spoke of him with real affection. 'He was such a man of the world but in the end liked nothing better than to come to sleep here at Ranvali, alone with the sea and the breeze, away from people, away from talkers, away from all the tangles of the town. He came every chance he got, every week, alone. It was a safe place for his spirit,' Carolis said.

I was surprised. I knew father had liked Ranvali but I didn't know he had come so often.

When mother died I was sent away to be looked after by Auntie Hema; I didn't see much of him then, but I always thought that was because he was busy with his politics. Father was a communist. I never thought it might be because he was at Ranvali staring out at the sea.

Father became a communist in his thirties. He was a quiet man, a big man, not easily influenced but once he decided on something he stuck to it, and I had thought he stuck to this thing, in his own way, until he died.

From the beginning father had lived in a mansion in the heart of our old town. It had tall elegant pillars and a porch that could accommodate a tank. He inherited it from his father and I was born in it. When he became a communist, it was there that he chose to announce his conversion.

Our huge dark dining-room had polished wood panels and grand arched bevelled mirrors at either end. There was a long *punkha*—an embroidered cloth screen with gold tassels—that hung over the length of the dining table, twenty foot at least, gently fanning the air, pulled by Podiyan on the veranda heaving on a cord like a bell-ringer; the poor boy—my buffalo when we played farm—rowed and sweated outside to cool the room. The whole family—uncles, aunts and cousins—had gathered around the table to celebrate some feast. One fat woman, who smelled of stale rice and eau-de-Cologne, kept pinching my cheek with huge purple nails and cooing. Suddenly father cut through all the talk in a crisp tense voice: 'What this country needs is a revolution,' he said, 'a *communist* revolution!' There was absolute silence. He slowly turned his knife in the air like a sword. I can see the light from the chandelier flashing off the blade even now, and a soldier's red uniform, black boots, gold spurs, horsemen charging across the Steppes. 'It is time for real change, this government is so clueless!' he said and all the family laughed as if he'd made a big joke. But I remember being tremendously proud of the way he silenced everybody at first, just like that.

Father was not one for big speeches. He didn't much like talking but that night he was right in the middle of it all. It was the first time I heard the word *communist*. It cast such a spell. I was only a child.

Some time after that he visited Moscow and brought back pictures of Red Square, snow covering everything, and the five communist stars above the Kremlin. Father said 'Look, these are ruby stars!' All my childhood I invested everything in Moscow with a fantastic bright ruby red. Ruby was my stone: it promised so much. When Marco Polo came here he was given a ruby the size of his arm: he was so impressed he wrote about nothing else in his journal. I used to wonder whether father had taken our rubies to Russia to make their stars, to cast a heavenly light on earth and turn the whole world red. Father kept his pictures in a large thick album. Each photograph was mounted with silver corners on black paper and neatly captioned with fine white copper-plate writing. I used to search it regularly for clues about this mysterious Russian magic of father's. I wanted to know what it was about it that had made him so notorious in our family circle, but there was no way of getting to the truth behind the pictures.

From that visit he also brought back a small Russian doll—a *matryoshka* doll. It was the only doll I really liked as a child. There were six of them, one inside the other. I especially liked the last doll, the innermost tiniest doll. She had a blue shawl painted over her head and the saddest eyes I had ever seen. The round black eyes and perfect eyebrows of the mother dolls turned into two black drips like tears on that last tiny shiny brown face. A fleck of red paint made a mouth through which she spoke to me about her country. I imagined a wonderful happy place full of children and horses and gilded carriages. A place where all families were large families. I thought my little doll was sad because she was homesick, and I imagined I was too. I tried to marry my father's feeling for Russia with snippets of admiration for things Russian I heard from other people: the Bolshoi, Tchaikovsky, Pushkin. I thought it was all the same thing, all part of the October Revolution that his friends would talk about sometimes when they came to our house and started drinking. All one big wonderful circus full of foreign light and life, sparkling and bubbling and lit by my rubies. My father never explained anything more. Maybe he thought that I knew all I needed to know. Or maybe he didn't know himself. Russia for us was just a place a long way away, like Ranvali.

I don't think father ever understood what a real *revolution* was despite what he said. He was so taken with the notion of the masses. It was absurd because it was impossible for him to really relate to them; he hardly spoke any Sinhala and no Tamil and his English was like a schoolmaster's. But he was anxious to do something. So he gave away money, bits and pieces from the house, anything that was at hand whenever anyone came to him. His friends loved his generosity and encouraged him. Mother tried hard to stop him. 'What about your daughter? What will be left for her?' She pushed me in front of him.

He did give so much away. Only the mansion itself he kept for us to live in, and that was because mother simply would not allow him to meddle with it. Mother was never impressed by father's communist talk. She thought he was naïve, an innocent, but she didn't think he'd come to any harm. She did her best to protect her own interests while allowing father to indulge in his ideological fantasy. Mother knew much better than he did about what makes the world tick, but she was too caught up in trying to defend our property. To her that was the most important thing: to own the roof over her head and keep some money in the till. She was pragmatic but frustrated by the way things were turning out. Whenever I ran to her she would put her hand to her eyes and complain 'Not now please . . . not now.' She was so mesmerized by the need to keep her own life in some meaningful shape.

Although she got her way with father over the house she had to give in on the garden: she had to let him turn the back garden—almost an acre of prime town-land—into a *gama*, a village of itinerants, a floating population that seemed to drift in from all over the country to camp in our backyard. 'Where do they all come from?' she'd ask and try to control the flood by cultivating border plants and marking out her ground rules. She grew crotons and high red-spiked cannas and somehow kept a real separation between the mansion and this village in the heart of our old town. She didn't trust any of them out there.

For father the *gama* was his precious link to the peasants, his masses, even though they treated him like a lord. They brought him pineapple and *jak*-fruit, plantains, *jaggery* and curd while he sat on the veranda rubbing his bare feet against each other in the afternoon sun looking more and more like Tolstoy than his Lenin. His feet, his arms, his elbows were always white with dry dead skin that he flaked off; small clouds of beautiful motes swirling in the sun's beam. I used to imagine there was no flesh to him, only layers and layers of skin which would peel in long mandalas in a slowly disintegrating roll of crude magic paper. Sometimes he would lean against a doorway and rub his back on an edge making the wood creak. He'd survey the land before him, deep in thought, but he never learned what was really happening in the *gama*. He had no idea about the *kasippu* stills—the moonshine—the ganja garden, the opium trade, the big black economy at the back of the house. For all father's sympathies we never set foot in the compound and it was only after he died and I took over the house that I discovered what was going on. I had to call the police in to clear out the place before I could sell up. There was no alternative. I had to sell the house to pay the estate-duties. Bills swarmed in from everywhere: money for this, money for that, lawyers' fees, taxes. I dreaded the postman. And because of the vagrants at the back, our house was seen as the source of all the trouble in town. I felt so sad for father. He would have been horrified. He really believed that people did things only for the best of reasons. Injustice and exploitation were unfortunate things to him, like accidents. I think his idea of a revolution was something like a gentleman's agreement to rearrange the furniture. He thought everyone agreed inequality was wrong and expected the rich to politely give up their comforts for the greater good as soon as they were asked.

'You are asking them to give up the things that they cherish,' mother shouted at him one day.

Father looked mystified. 'What cherishing?' All they had, to him, were a few unappreciated privileges.

'But what for? Why should they? Why should we give up what we have for heaven's sake? It didn't come from nowhere . . . '

Father dismissed her arguments with a wave of his large dry speckled hand. 'For the country my dear. It will make us strong and unified. Otherwise . . . ' He spread out his arms ' . . . it will be pitiful.' His face was so long and sombre. I used to think he could see into the heart of things. He wanted a bloodless revolution: a change in the way we all lived brought about by a shift in our minds. He thought each of us could improve the lives around us before we died, and that we should. *Let a hundred flowers blossom.* It was as simple as that.

When the Insurgency happened, in 'seventy-one, it must

have been a great shock for him. The bloodshed. That
April changed everything. The bodies of hundreds of
young boys choked the rivers for weeks. The water turned
red. They wanted a revolution: young and angry and now
forever dead. Father's friends would have known some of
those activists; they might have been to our house
drinking coffee into the early hours of the morning,
arguing: why didn't he see what was coming? Thuggery,
goondas, terrorism. Was he so out of touch? Maybe he had
left all these things behind by then; perhaps he dreamed
only of his Ranvali, his sea and his sand, his sleep; grateful
for forgetting; growing *in* like the trees around the
bungalow.

That night at Ranvali I began to see father as a different
man from the one I had always imagined. Not the
communist, not even the idealist, but a brooding old man
just looking for some peace and quiet; a hole to sleep in
by himself. But I wanted to find him: all his thoughts, all
his furniture that I sold. I wanted to turn out the almirahs,
empty the drawers again, go through everything; walk the
same pathways, sleep in the same rooms, somehow pick up
some trace of him. I wanted to see his face, his face when I
was born. The young man he was. The boy. I wanted to see
him as a baby. Once I saw him in the doorway of mother's
room. The light by the bed was on. His bare body was
yellow in front and black behind. His head was bowed, he
looked crestfallen. There was a thread—a white cotton
thread with a silver amulet that some soothsayer had told
him to wear—around his waist. Then he must have closed
the door, or she turned out the light. Or maybe I fell
asleep. He whispered something that I couldn't hear. Was
he frightened of me? Or was he ashamed of me?
Embarrassed at being a father?

It was almost midnight when I eventually fell asleep,
even though I was exhausted. I slept badly. The dark was

always disturbing when I was a child. My room always seemed full of marauders. I would freeze under the sheets.

When I woke up I felt my mind had been mauled. I am not superstitious: I don't believe in spirits and omens; bad dreams are bad dreams not newspapers, but I felt awful. I felt awful about father and my feelings about him. I felt awful about the dead children in the river, about Carolis, his life, and the boy who cut the *thambili*. I felt awful about my own life. I got out of bed and banged open the shutters. I stuck my head out and shook it to get all the awfulness out. I wanted to go to the beach again. I pulled on a kimono.

Carolis was in the backyard scraping half a coconut for breakfast. The pure white grated coconut had fallen in a perfect cone-shaped mound on the plate under the scraper. 'Morning tea?' he asked.

'Maybe later.' The wind had picked up. I followed the sandy path up to the rusty barbed wire fence and the small wooden gate facing the ocean. Beyond it was a patch of thick green sea-creepers and then the beach. The surf boomed.

There was a storm brewing. I sat by an old outrigger and watched the dark clouds boiling on the horizon begin to bunch up into angry blue-black fists.

The first thunder rolled when I was back in the bungalow having my tea. It was a long low rumble. Then suddenly everything went dark. There was a streak of lightning and a loud explosion. A huge coconut frond crashed down in the garden. A big bucket tipped. Thunder exploded behind the bungalow and the garden disappeared in a sheet of silver water. Rain bounced in huge drops onto the veranda and splattered like bullets on the roof, the trees, the sand. Clattering, hammering, digging holes in the ground. The sound drowned out even the ocean.

When I was little I would strip off and run out in the rain to dance and jump up and down. But I was never allowed to go in the sea when it was raining, as if there was something especially dangerous about getting wet from the sea and the sky at the same time: two whirlpools grabbing both head and foot.

At the first flash of lightning near the bungalow Carolis had quickly covered all the mirrors and hidden all the cutlery, every bit of moveable metal. He shoved them all inside cupboards and under the beds so the lightning wouldn't hit us.

When the rain eventually stopped it was late afternoon. It looked as though the storm had moved on. I wanted to leave for home immediately, but first had to inspect everything with Carolis to check for damage the way father would have done. The whole place was flooded. Lots of young coconuts were down and plenty of branches, but fortunately only one tree had been hit. 'They are good trees,' Carolis said, 'They know how to bend.'

The bungalow itself had not been damaged much; only some of the roof tiles had been lifted.

By the time I was ready to leave a low sinking pink sun had broken through the clouds briefly and the puddles of rain water glistened. I said goodbye to Carolis and the boy, beeping the horn for them as I set off back up the muddy lane.

On the main road I drove leaning forward, embracing the wheel, lifting myself up to see further, to go faster. It was late and I felt a little anxious about driving home in the dark. But inside the car the sound of the engine was hypnotic. Every now and again storm showers returned to hammer the vehicle. It was as if the storm was attacking the coast in waves: it would pass, I'd catch up and overtake it only to meet it again around the next turn; the rain would rattle over the car and I'd go faster and faster.

The trees lining the road became silhouettes. A gilt line divided the sky from the edge of the sea: everything else was turning black. Then I came around a bend and a fire flared on the road ahead. I touched the brakes and slowed down. There was a makeshift road-block of oil-drums and logs laid across. A red flag was up.

Some figures moved at the edge of the road and two young men came slowly towards the car. I wound down my window. 'What's the matter?'

The man in front, the leader, looked hard at me. He had a wispy beard and a long thin throat. When he swallowed I could see his Adam's apple plummet. He was dressed in a jungle shirt and blue trousers. He shone a torch on me. There was some whispering in the dark. Someone climbed on to one of the oil-drums on the road. He cupped his hands and lit a cigarette. A red glowing face floated in the air.

'What's happening here?' I asked again.

The man beckoned to another figure. I think he was surprised to see me—a woman driving alone at night.

Father—*Thaththi*—died on this coast road. His Austin had hit the rocks by the open railway crossing. He had been such a good driver . . . He was the one who first taught me to drive. He was wonderful then. He used to sit me on his lap behind the wheel and let me steer. I couldn't go wrong. I could feel his warm breath against my ear, his hands guiding the wheel 'Keep it steady . . . a little to the left . . . ' In the car he knew who he was, he could hold me and speak to me. It was outside, when he got out of the driving seat, that he didn't know what to do with me. Maybe in his eyes I too was turning into something he couldn't understand.

After some whispering the man with the beard turned around and waved me through. I went into gear and put my foot down hard on the accelerator; I almost hit one of the oil drums as the car leapt but I didn't care. I wasn't going to let up until I reached home. All the way I kept wondering about Ranvali and about father—his dream, and my dreams—and what he would have done if he had been in the car with me.

CARAPACE

ANURA PERERA IS coming over tonight. *Amma*—my mother —says I ought to take him seriously. I told Vijay about it.

So?

He's coming to see me because he is interested in me and he has serious intentions. He lives in Australia!

Vijay grinned and said nothing. That's the way with Vijay.

Do you know who Anura Perera is?

He shook his head, no. Then he laughed, So he's looking for a Lankan wife?

Yes! I said. Anura Perera has a dollar job, a Sydney house, and an Australian ticket.

So what are you saying? Vijay laughed. You are going to marry this prick with a foreign job? Is that what you've come to tell me?

That wasn't what I had come to tell him at all. I first met Vijay at the new disco. It was a birthday party and there was a crowd of about twenty people in our group. I didn't know many of them. My friend Lakshmi took me along to it. It was her friend's birthday but we had all been waiting to go to this new place. Everyone was talking about it. It was packed out that night. The dance floor was fabulous: round, with lights flashing underneath and all sorts of fantastic gadgets turning around the room. Vijay was not in our party. He came up to me and said, How about a dance? I could hardly hear him, but I could see his mouth in the dark. And when the lights flashed on him I could see him looking straight at me like he really wanted to dance with me. We danced all night. He bought me rum and coke and smoked lots of cigarettes. In the end he asked whether we could meet again.

Only the next day I discovered he is the cook at the Beach Hut. He is older than me; tall and long and always smiling. He has such a mop of hair and is so skinny. He never eats! He says he likes to see his food eaten by other people. To watch his customers, his friends, grow fat and happy. He says there is nothing he likes better than to stir his pan of squid in front of the ocean. His face is big and square like a bony box stretched over with skin; his lips barely keep his teeth in and he always seems about to burst into a laugh. And when he does the whole sea seems to crease up. The beach is so lovely with him.

When I went to see him today he said hello with a big grin on his face. Come sit down, I won't be long. He had a basin full of enormous prawns on his lap. *Loku isso*, he said.

A newspaper spread out on the floor under him was heaped with plucked prawn heads and shells. Orange whiskers. After peeling each prawn he carefully pulled out a thin blue vein that curved around it like a backbone. Look at that, he held the vein up: sea-poison.

At first I didn't even want to open my mouth about Anura Perera, but *Amma* says you must always go for the best you can. And I know Anura Perera will come in a big Mitsubishi, air-conditioned with tinted glass and a stereo. I wanted Vijay to know.

When he finished with the prawns he washed his hands and poured out some coffee for me. What are we going to do? I asked. I wanted to know what he really felt for me.

About what?

About us, I said. What are we going to do?

He said, There's an American film at the Majestic.

It is so easy for him. He doesn't see anything. There are no problems, no hang-ups. He's not like the other guys around here, always trying something on. He comes straight out with what he thinks. But I must have looked worried; he leaned forward. What is it you want to know then? he asked, touching my hand. He has such a light touch. His fingernails are like sea-shells, slightly pink, with little half-moons peeping out. When he touches my hand with his fingers I feel tremendous and I want to go on like this for ever, just drinking coffee together and looking at the sea.

I told him we've got to sort things out. Going to the pictures won't solve anything.

But you like movies, he said.

For months nothing has happened and now suddenly everything happens: Vijay first, now Anura Perera. When *Amma* talks to me I see a whole new world. I don't think Vijay could even imagine it. He would just laugh. *Amma* said we could go and buy a new saree. Something really nice. And I saw just the shoes at Tonio's, next to the supermarket. Imagine flying, stopping in Singapore! I can't believe it but it is what I've dreamed of all along; something happening so I can be someone instead of this crazy feeling that nothing matters. But then when I go to Vijay I really don't know what I want . . .

He looked at me and clicked his tongue, So what matters so much? He lit one of his thin crackly cigarettes and stretched out on his chair. His head rested on the back of it; he let his mouth stay open like a fish gulping. Sometimes he can be so idiotic!

But it isn't that simple. It isn't! We can't just stay like this, I said. The Beach Hut isn't going to be here for ever. The bamboo and coconut will split. The wood on the window-frame is already rising, turning itself inside out. I looked out of the doorway and watched the green sandy water of the ocean swelling and falling. You can't be a beach cook for the rest of your life, I said. Or is that all you want? Do you really only want to be a *cook* all your life? I didn't want to upset him, I just wanted him to say something; but he just stared at me. He looked at me as if I were way out at sea, already floating across the ocean. But who is the drifter? Not me.

A crowd of bathers turned up looking for beer and his beach *roti*, so I said I better go; he had work to do. I asked him to call me as soon as he could, before evening. It is important. Call me, *please*. He smiled sweetly and nodded OK. Then he screwed up his eyes and sucked the last of his smoke through his fingers and held it in his chest.

At home everyone was busy. I came to my room and stayed out of the way. I wanted to be alone. Nobody seemed to miss me. By five o'clock, when I looked out, the whole place was dusted and tidied up; the floor in the front room has been polished and Auntie Manel has even brought flowers for that ghastly green vase that sits by the telephone. The house is filled with a kind of sea musk. *Amma* has made sandwiches and *patties* and roasted cashew nuts spiced with red chilli to put out in her special silver bowl. I have never seen the place looking like this.

Amma has been having palpitations; I know she has been rushing around all over the place arranging everything, her breasts heaving with excitement. She is so anxious, but it's no accident that this first meeting is happening tonight; she would have consulted her astrologer. She wouldn't have taken any risks! It must be the most auspicious day of the month. I suppose I should make a fuss and ask her: Do I have a choice in all of this? But I don't want to choose. I hate choosing.

It's all so crazy. What's in Australia anyway? Everyone wants to go there, especially when there's any disturbance here. But what for? I like the beach here. I like our road, our bougainvillaea slumping over the wall and that sandy walk we go on across the railway tracks down to the sea. I like the disco. I like going by *putt-putt* yellow three-wheelers. Just to live in a large fancy bungalow with a view of the Opera House or something! What's so great about that? Vijay would say it's all in the head.

If only he would turn up with something. But *Amma* would die if she knew about him. She'd throw a fit. A cook on the beach! What she wants to say is . . . Good evening Mr Perera, so pleased to meet you. Do come and take my daughter away; transform her world with your brilliance—and your nice fat bank account. Give her a modern house, a big car, fancy clothes, shoes she can afford to throw away after every party. Give her expensive things, and by-the-by your unswerving respect, and all will be well. She will be an asset to your career, a pearl in your crown. Just take her Mr Perera, please take her to Australia away from here, and don't forget her mother . . . *Anura.*

I waited and waited for Vijay to call. I didn't know what I wanted him to say, but I thought he would find something. He wouldn't let things slip just for the want of a few words. Then about an hour ago the telephone rang. I let it ring for a bit. *Amma* was in the bathroom. Nobody else answers the telephone in our house. Eventually I picked it up. I was so nervous I could hardly speak.

What time can you come out to eat tonight? Vijay asked. I've made a special dish: *fantastic*, with those big prawns!

I could hear the ocean in the telephone. I could see him with a big grin on his face, pulling open his white shirt and rubbing his bare bony chest with his long fingers. He'd have the lamps lit under the trees.

I said, I can't talk; the iron is on. I was ironing my jade-green saree, the one that *Amma* bought for me. I told him, I have to put the phone down. I put it down. He won't ring again. He thinks I know his number by heart: Mount Lavinia 926979, 926979.

STRAW HURTS

Tɪssᴀ ʜᴀs ᴀ hard hardboard bed. A straw mat curling up at the edges frayed maroon and blue. Diamond weaves in and out. His room is dark and cool; the floor uneven, with four chalky lime-green walls rising and a high cross-beam. By the door the mirror is small and round with the sky floating. Underneath he has fixed a shelf for his bottle of red king-coconut hair-oil and his two-edged razor. From his bed you can watch the colours tear in the mirror, the sun slicing on the smashed bottle-glass embedded in the curved top of the roadside cement wall and sinking.

The room opens to a narrow backyard. At one end, by the washroom, is a clump of plantain trees and a patch of tall sword-leaf ginger. Row upon row of small sweet yellow pipes with their dark tips pursed swell in a carriage, the heavy purple flower—a big velvet cone—points at the ground, swivelling open. A thin half-moon open drain runs the length of the building: a six-second burst, running barefoot.

On this side of the wall is our house; in our backyard there is nothing. Nothing but red dust and round-headed black ants streaming and one juicy banana trunk stabbed brown—jab jab jab—never dead. I am always looking over the wall for Tissa.

113

2

Sundown; head down I hear him go to the washroom.

I call out, Tissa! Tissa!

Come over, come come, he says.

He squats by a large metal pail and uses a small plastic bowl to pour water on himself. Dries, rubs talcum powder all over; his cheeks and neck turn pasty. He wraps a white sarong around him, snaps a black vinyl belt with a silver clasp and buttons a pearly shirt; combs his short wiry hair hard. He lights three joss-sticks and sticks them in a cake of sandalwood on a wooden shrine in the far corner of the room. The little platform is strewn with marigolds, yellow temple-flowers; there is a buddha sitting lotus-position and a small white bell of a *stupa* with a brass spire. The air is rich: the smell of incense, straw and oil, quickly dying hot moist flowers, his man's hair. Powder petals crush at the touch. Indigo and saffron, blue-paste crumbles on the wood. He murmurs a prayer, long-lashed eyelids fluttering shut and his fingers drumming on each other. His large crumpled lips unpleat making tiny bubbles. His mouth is supple. Outside above us the evening is streaked with pink clouds.

Where are you going? Can I come?

Come, come to the *kadé*, he says, the tea kiosk at the top of the road.

3

In the early evening, at twilight, our road bursts into life. For a little while all around pinks, greens, reds and blues, whites brighten; crows circle in hundreds cawing at the black sky; the sound of cars, bicycle bells, cows, voices become loud. Grow louder. Everything is magnified from the inside. Open wet sticky cow-lips suck and feed; cycle spokes, stars and street lights sparkle, marking the edge of what you can see. Fox-bats flap and bitterns hide in rice fields, a shrieking *ulama*—the devil-bird—calls *buku buku buku koa*. Stories nest like serpents in the head of the *Pissa*, the mad boy, our half-wit, who walks sparking out of his mouth—*pissa pissa pissa*—jittering he picks up a tin, rattles it, hurls it at the startled red tail of a passing car. Our night-life, our main road . . .

I'm coming, wait. I go back over the wall for my knife. I carry it always out on the road now. A small sharp knife that folds into itself. I tuck it in my waistband under my shirt. Cool comfort, lethal. The whetstone gives a clean ·hard rasp. My small god of protection.

4

Tissa says in his village there was a well. From the well a *yakkha*, a demon, bit him when he lifted the bucket to bathe. He has tooth-marks on him to show: the four round fang-holes of a well-demon. They had to perform an exorcism and do penance all night; afterwards go to temple for a formal *pirith* blessing. The *bhikkus* droned for hours *buddham saranam gachchami, dhammam saranam gachchami, sangham saranam gachchami* . . . three times three . . . I take refuge, I take refuge, I take refuge . . . their shaven heads nodding. He had a fever for three days, there was so much in his past for him to atone for. In the end he left home and came here.

He stuck a peacock feather in the ground and called it his insurance. He laughs now, quietly.

5

At the *kadé* two men are in a pool of street-light with their sarongs half hitched up, the night air cooling their legs. One of them, Lokka, the bigger man, pinned me

115

against a wall one night, pressing hard. He wormed into my thighs and jiggled his fat legs, jerking. He has a fat layer of scum under his skin and a rat's mouth. I could feel his scummy head burst.

Here he comes! he says. Tissa and his shrimp.

The other man turns. Cigarette?

So what's happening?

Nothing. We are just waiting.

The kiosk is lit by a dim yellow bulb. Behind the vendor's cubicle are big gallon jars of sweets and spices and rows of cigarette packets: *Gold Leaf, Three Roses*. In front the zinc-top counter is flanked by a betel box and stacks of heart-shaped green *bulath* leaves neatly stacked stem on stem, groove on groove. On one side a long smouldering wick hangs for customers to light their cigarettes and dry-rolled *beedis*. Tissa raps the counter with a coin and a sleepy man appears from a hole in the back. A glass of tea?

The man brings out two thick fluted glasses. He lifts a large kettle simmering on the oil stove and pours tea boiled with condensed milk into a glass. Then holding a glass in each hand he pours the tea from glass to glass in a yard long stream as if pulling yarn. Shadows jump like puppets around the inside of the shack. I see a monster with a garrotte of tea. When he has an inch of froth he places the glass in front of Tissa and flicks the coin into his purse. He wipes the zinc with a grimy rag.

Tissa picks up the hot glass by the rim holding it between the tips of his thumb and forefinger.

I wish we could walk away but Tissa wants to talk. He turns to the other two and asks about the rally.

Usual stuff, Lokka says. He ignores me as if I didn't exist. I shrink more and more until it feels like there's nothing there.

We *must* win . . .

Lokka grunts. You tell them *machang*, you tell them we must win. His face is bulbous; an ugly devil mask.

Tissa lights another cigarette off the wick. His face is masked in smoke. I have three votes here, he whispers; his eyes are gleaming drunk.

Here! Three?

Yes. Also two in another district.

The third man, Huna, shakes his head in disbelief. How?

I told you, we have to win.

But how?

Preparation my friend. I registered in different places. I've got all the numbers now. Your two votes, my one here, and five extra. Eight altogether!

Huna, the gecko, makes a stupid *chuk-chuk-chuk*.

I'll do three, and you can also do three, and Lokka two. Right?

The other two look blank. But how can you vote in three places?

I told you. I have the numbers.

Idiot. *Gona.* You think they'll let you do that? This is an election not a circus you know. They mark you so that you can't cheat. Lokka gloats as if he knows everything.

It can be rubbed off.

It can't. They won't have ink you just rub off.

I'm telling you I can get it off. I will get it off in half an hour. I *will.*

With your juice? Lokka laughs uglily, scratching at his crotch.

Tissa jumps up. *Ado!* He lifts up his hand palm stretched open as if to slap him. I know what I'm talking about!

I urge him on silently. Hit him, hit him hard. Kick him in his fat groin.

Look my friend, Lokka tilts his thick head back, in

your village maybe you can use chicken shit and jungle magic but this is the real world. That stuff doesn't work here, you understand?

So Lokka, our big chief, is frightened? Too frightened to vote!

I'm not frightened of a blue spot, but what's the point? You want to run around the countryside for this election —what for? What's in it for us?

6

Walking back home I ask Tissa why he didn't hit my enemy.

What for?

He's bad. Did you see his ear? His left ear is missing a bit, I nicked it with a knife. He said bad things about my mother: *I could have killed him.* I used the kitchen knife, you know. He hit me with a stick. He hit the knife shouting, but I held it tight. I didn't drop it. I was wild. I jumped him from all sides. I went for him. I went for him wild until I drew blood. He got such a shock. He put his hand to his head and found blood. His pukey blood.

You mustn't be so stupid. A man like Lokka, he is too big to fight, Tissa whispers into my ear. I feel his tongue right in my ear.

But he was scared, I could have killed him.

Then what?

Then nothing, I said. Rats like him . . . Who needs them?

Tissa strokes my head in the dark. *Aney putha,* you are too young to talk like that.

But I feel so angry. The filth he spouted. His hands around me. Now if he comes close again, I have a knife that can't be stopped . . .

7

Manike is awake, sifting rice-flour for tomorrow's breakfast.

You're back early, she says when Tissa opens the screen door into her kitchen. It is the way in to his room at the back.

We only went to meet the boys.

Those two layabouts?

We were talking politics.

Not getting yourself into trouble, please? Not with this child. She points at me with a wooden spoon.

No no no. What trouble? You know our party has to win. You'll be voting for us won't you?

Me? I don't care any more. What difference does it make? Whoever wins, my life will not change.

She must be in her seventies. No one knows her real age. She has always been there. In the fluorescent light her skin hangs in flat pouches around her eyes, around her mouth, around her neck. Even her elbows have big folds of leathery skin. The skin is dusted with flour. Her teeth are rotten.

But *amma*, we have to win, to change the world.

What for? You talk such foolishness. But you do what you think is right. That's all right. She shakes her head from side to side. Whatever happens we end up with what we deserve. Our *karuma*.

We'll see, Tissa steps outside. *Karma, karuma, karma.* We will see. He lights another cigarette and flicks the match into the drain.

8

Tissa has thirteen marbles for me. One is huge and spotted and fills my palm, but the others are neat plain colours twisted into feathers in the glass. Each feather has a cleft. We play on the sandy ground outside his room. A square scratched out with a twig; a dimple in the middle and ten paces marked off for me and twelve for him. He has a long reach, but I beat him. He clicks his tongue loudly and slaps his thigh every time I make a hit. I skip.

It's so easy; it's so easy.

9

Next day I look for him but his door is closed, locked with a padlock. But there is a gap to look in through. Not there, he is nowhere.

I wait and wait; nothing happens. I chase the crows off our roof. When it gets dark the *karapoththas* come out. I see a pair of feelers first, then the long brown shiny shield of a roach's body scrambles out of the drain-hole and darts into the house. And then another. I hunt them.

Later I notice his light come on and I climb over the wall. The backyard is dark except for this one square of yellow light slammed out of his room. It's a hot night; the air is on fire.

Inside the joss-sticks are smoking: long thin blue lines all the way up to the ceiling. A shirt hangs lifeless on a clothes-line in a corner. Two clay lamps, small and oil-rubbed, burn.

He is on his small wooden stool, smoking.

Where have you been?

He blows three smoke-rings quickly one after the other, each one chasing the previous one and going through and through each other.

Did you win?

He shows a thumb imprinted with a big blue spot. I couldn't get it off. It was impossible.

I examine the mark. The ink makes the lines on the flesh much more distinct. I see each ridge curling round in ever decreasing odd shaped rings. My mother can read palms; I am learning.

I don't think I could have done it anyway, he says almost to himself. I should cut it off.

What about the other two? Lokka and Huna?

They didn't want to know. They are not even going to try.

Will you tell them what happened? *Don't. Don't.* I don't want him to be laughed at by Lokka. That bastard would laugh so loud at Tissa's blue thumb. I don't want that to happen. You don't need to tell them anything, do you?

10

It was only an idea, that was all, he says to me. I wanted to do the best I could; but it was a waste of time. His head sinks.

There is nothing wrong then is there? I pull at a piece of loose dyed straw from his mat and a whole line of maroon comes out. There are big holes where it has unravelled: bent bits prick my skin.

No problem.

Nothing at all?

I feel an ill mist hurting in the room.

Thanikama, he says—meaning he is alone, almost.

He pushes me, Go home, he says. It's late. Your mother will be looking for you.

MONKFISH MOON

PETER WAS A Colombo business magnate: fifty-nine, grossly overweight, short. He looked as though he had never moved. Monsoons came and went, governments toppled, the country lurched from left to right, but he remained untouched in his swivel-chair, holding audience with a cigarette in one hand, a whisky-soda in the other and a vast stomach in between. Peter had the world at his fingertips.

But if there was money to be made anywhere in town he would be there: he missed nothing. Under the socialists he prospered helping the young republic hustle its way, and when they lost control and the economy was freed Peter again prospered as the king of the market. Even in times of calamitous trouble—the Insurgency of 'seventy-one, the Eelam war of the Tamil Tigers—Peter never lost a cent. And now with the south erupting again in People's Liberation and the ultra-conservative rear guard—the Green Tigers—out on the rampage, Peter seemed richer than ever. The only deterioration was that he was beginning to age. His round face had become distinctly flabby and his heavy jowls pulled the lower lids of his eyes down to give him a permanently red-rimmed look; his skin was grey. He breathed slowly, noisily.

'In this country now everybody is frightened.' He leaned forward in his chair like a mountain tipping. He looked at me searching my face. 'Do you know why they are frightened?'

'The uncertainty of everything?'

'No, I'll tell you why. They are frightened because they feel guilty. They feel guilty for all the things they have done and all the things they haven't done. For all the little lies they have told, the adulteries they have committed. For not doing the right thing, for doing the wrong thing. For all this shooting and burning . . . ' he lifted his head up. 'Guilty people are frightened people. They think their time is now up.'

'What about you? No fear?'

A low laugh rumbled in his belly and burbled up to his lips. 'I have no guilt, whatever people may say I have nothing to hide. So I have nothing to fear! Anyway all these damn fools need me.'

I was first introduced to Peter by my uncle who knew him from his school-days. Whenever I visited my uncle he would talk about Peter's exploits and successes: his cloves, the famous Bombay onion shipment, his guava juice venture, and his many flamboyant love affairs. He was a folk-hero to us all.

As a young man Peter had written poetry, read philosophy and practised ballroom dancing. He was constantly in love. Early in the nineteen-fifties he came into an inheritance: a large plot of virgin land which he planted with coconut, rice, clove and other spices. His timing was perfect; with every harvest prices rose and rose. Peter grew immensely rich. He learned to love the growth of money. My uncle said that in those early days Peter was quite a slim young man, but success larded that modest frame layer by layer changing his shape like the contours of a growing town until one day he discovered his belly completely hid his feet from his eyes. But he never grew complacent. Month in and month out, over the decades, Peter regularly visited his plantations and tramped around the paddy fields and clove gardens. 'The best manure for an estate is the owner's footsteps,' he would say and march about barking orders, shooting snipe.

I met Peter myself only after my uncle was posted back to Colombo. I used to visit him there from time to time and he took me to see Peter. I had expected Peter to be an aloof and busy man, but I found him surprisingly interested in me. He liked us and I learned to enjoy talking to him.

Peter swung around in his chair and reached for his desk with one hand. A fat grey thumb hooked onto the top while his short puffy index finger pressed a white button screwed onto the belly of the desk. Somewhere in the depths of the house a buzzer served out his summons.

'Look, you must stay to dinner,' he said commanding me as much as inviting me.

I hadn't seen Peter for almost five years. That evening I had just dropped in to say that I was back in town. While I was thinking of what to do a breathless young woman came to the door. Peter looked at her out of the corner of his eye. He rubbed the palms of his hands together making a rasping sound and softly informed her that there was going to be a dinner party in an hour or two; he spoke looking down at his stomach without turning towards her.

The woman stared at him with her lips drawn in. She said nothing. She leaned against the doorway and pulled at her thick coarse hair tied in a bun at the back of her head.

Eventually Peter looked up at her and took a deep noisy breath. This seemed to mark a slight change in the proceedings and he, rather more sternly, started issuing instructions for the meal. He looked at me. 'What do you like to eat? Fish? Pork? String-hoppers?'

I shrugged and said, 'Anything.' I was going to stay.

The woman suddenly started talking rapidly in such an odd high-pitched voice that I couldn't follow her.

'Crabs! You'll like some crabs? Chandrani says some chap has brought crabs . . . ' Peter said to me and broke into a violent coughing fit that seemed to scrape out the inside of his lungs. The woman, Chandrani, seemed unconcerned. As she did nothing, I waited too. He stopped as suddenly as he had started. He took some short angry breaths but then talked as if nothing had happened '. . . crabs from Chilaw.'

'Fine,' I said. 'Chilaw crabs! Only *you* would just happen to have Chilaw crabs!'

He beamed for a moment, and then let his lower lip slowly droop in a fifty-nine-year-old child's pout. 'But they are not the best. It's full moon you know; they run around too much in the light. Lose weight, lose taste. For good meat you need a new moon.' He closed his eyes. I could imagine the deep water, a big heavy red moon with a sharp rim chasing weird sea-creatures across the ocean floor. Peter gave some more orders to Chandrani and when she finally retreated he turned to me. 'Have a drink,' he pointed at the trolley by the door. 'Help yourself to whatever you like. Scotch? She'll bring some ice in a minute.' When she returned with the bucket of ice he teased her. 'Chandrani thinks I drink too much. She dilutes the bottle! Silly woman thinks I don't notice.'

Chandrani reared back her head somehow managing to look both disdainful and indulgent at the same time.

'She thinks she is a bloody doctor, but she never even finished fifth grade.' Peter clicked an old silver lighter. 'Where's your doctor's certificate then?' he demanded looking up at her.

She wiped an ice-wet hand across her mouth and walked out of the room. She had obviously tended him for some time; she was used to his ways.

I poured the drinks and we talked about my travels. Every now and again he would flap his hand urging me to speak louder. 'Ah!' he would say widening his eyes at some innocuous remark of mine as if hearing only bits of what I said. He was unable to give anything his undivided attention. Our conversation, sometimes even sentences, would be interrupted by other conversations before being picked up again and continued. From time to time he would lift the telephone off its hook and dial some numbers while nodding patiently at whatever I happened to be saying. He would mumble a few words to someone on the other end of the line and put the receiver down. 'We must have a good party tonight!' he explained, smiling at me. There were several of these calls, last minute invitations, offering dinner to various people. All apparently gratefully accepted.

As the afternoon wore on his speech occasionally became slightly slurred; he looked immensely tired. I wondered if he should rest and suggested we cancel the dinner but he wouldn't hear of it. 'Nonsense!' he said and continued with his phone-calls.

I noticed how that beaming rotundity that once had been such an unmistakable sign of his good living now irredeemably sagged. The bounce had gone. It now very clearly signalled a neglected health. But he had always taken pride in being unconcerned with his health. He liked to turn hedonism on its head and say that he indulged himself not because of a craving but because of his total disregard for things of the flesh. If the body has no intrinsic value, why tend it so lovingly? To him it was a waste of time. If it meant nothing, then you might as well indulge in everything.

But after the final call he pushed the telephone away to the edge of his desk and for the first time seemed to weigh me up. He looked at me as if from a great distance and said in a slightly mocking voice that long ago when he was my age most of all he had wanted a spiritually pure life. He had really wanted to be a monk. To live in complete detachment on nothing but the poetry of the mind. I pictured him with a begging bowl and a black umbrella, his body a *dagoba* of eight-fold flesh: buried lotus legs, a three-tier seated stomach, round shoulders, a roll of a neck, a face smooth with contentment topped by a shaved dome. 'Yes,' I said, 'a monk of the good life!' But he claimed he would not even have worn a saffron robe because the dye would have seemed too rich. He looked down at his drink. 'But before you can chuck away the world like that, you have to have it in your hand, no?' He poked the ice in his glass with a thick stubby finger and then waved the wet finger at the antique Dutch furniture and pieces of carved ivory dotted around the room. His face was dead-pan. I never could tell how much he was having me on. 'You can't take it with you when you go, and the more you collect the more obvious it becomes. So now I keep these things to remind me of mortality . . . ' He let the words trail out of his boyish mouth. No doubt Peter had concluded many a business deal in his favour on precisely such a point of relative values. He had the knack for buying low and selling high. He cleared his throat and got to his feet pulling his sarong around his high floating belly. He looked vaguely distracted. A deep furrow appeared on his forehead and his breath quickened. 'Have another drink,' he commanded and waddled towards the door, 'I'll be back soon.'

I poured myself some plain soda and sipped it listening to the bubbles pipping the surface.

130

When he didn't return I went out into the hall and called out. There was no answer but Chandrani the servant woman heard me and came to the stairs.

'Ice?' she asked looking up at me from one of the lower steps. Her long thin back tightly covered in a white cotton bodice twitched as she crept up the steps in the dim light.

I said no, not ice, but I was wondering what had happened to Peter. I said I was worried because he had been gone so long.

She smiled pityingly and said he was just finishing his bath and that he would be out soon. Her long arms motioned me back into the room. He will be out soon, she repeated firmly. The bathroom and bedroom were further along the landing and I heard running water. I nodded and stepped back into the room feeling a little foolish, but it was a premonition.

When Peter finally returned he was dressed in a finely cut dark suit that lent even his bulk a real elegance. The shirt was cream coloured and had a soft collar that lay gently around his thick neck. He wore a black silk tie fastened with a amethyst tie-pin and had shaved and smoothed back his hair with pomade. As he made his way to his chair I caught the scent of an expensive after-shave.

I had never seen him dressed up like this before. I asked him whether he had invited someone very special to dinner.

He giggled juicily and sat down tapping another of his cigarettes on the back of a flip-top pack.

The guests came straight upstairs as they arrived. They knew their way in Peter's house.

'Oh my goodness Uncle, in a suit!' the first to arrive, a

young woman, exclaimed. Her husband, Ananda, said 'Very smart Uncle, what is the occasion?'

Peter chuckled and introduced me from his chair. 'It's a party, and tonight is full moon!'

'You must have won at the races or something,' Ananda said.

Peter clicked his tongue, 'Ah no, but tomorrow, maybe tomorrow . . . Anyway come, sit down and have a drink.'

Ananda went over to the trolley and poured out a drink for himself. His wife declined. 'No, no nothing for me just yet.' She shook her head vigorously and plumped herself down on the nearest chair.

'And where is your lovely daughter tonight?' Peter asked.

'We took her swimming today. So she went to sleep nice and early. Ayah is there.'

'A wonderful child,' Peter said to me. 'A truly wonderful child. If only . . .'

'What, Uncle?'

Peter rubbed both his cheeks with his hands. 'I would have liked to have seen her . . . '

His nephew turned to me. 'It is really quite something, Uncle is totally enraptured by Sushila. He will spend the whole day with her anytime he is given half a chance.'

'He'd make a wonderful ayah, no Ananda?'

Ananda laughed out aloud. 'You know the other day we came for lunch—when was it Shiromi? Saturday?'

'No Sunday, Sunday!'

'Anyway, we came for lunch and afterwards we were watching the video downstairs—that new movie—but Uncle was up here painting with Sushila all afternoon. Isn't that so Uncle?'

Peter had been studying the couple. He now permitted a small smile to reach his lips. 'She is only three years old, and such a wonderful child. I'd like to see her when she

grows up. But it will be the next century . . . ' He turned
back to his desk and opened a drawer. He pulled out a
sheaf of drawing paper. 'Look,' he handed them over to
me, 'these are her pictures . . . '

I leafed through them. Peter obviously wanted me to
see something in them that he did; the parents also were
expectant. 'Nice pictures,' I said. There were big bold
blue patches on most of the pieces of paper. One had a
circle smeared with red and yellow.

'The sea' Peter said. 'That's the sea with fish swimming.
And the circle is the moon!'

I said I thought it was a man: a bald red head and a
wonderful big fat blue body.

Peter took the pictures back and carefully put them
away in his drawer. No one said anything else for a
moment and it seemed as though we were all
contemplating the paintings. Then more people arrived.

The place filled up with voices. The Weerasinghes, Lal
and Kamala, Lester Disanayake, and Anton Kularatna the
fixer, all arrived at the same time. I didn't know the
Weerasinghes but the other two I had met before.

Peter remained seated on his swivel chair by the desk.
The rest of us perched in an awkward semicircle before
him. Lester, a lawyer who had been at college with Peter,
began talking about a mutual friend. He removed his
spectacles from his face and pinched the bridge of his
nose as if he were slowly bursting a small memory of
their friend. 'Who would have expected it. The fellow
was totally abstemious. Even in Varsity days—not a drop.
The fellow had never had a drink in his life. And no
smoking also. No smoking, no liquor, and yet a stroke
came out of the blue. Dr Jayawardene told me that this
blood clot can happen any time. Just bad luck! You see,
the clot had travelled along the blood vessels out of the
lung to the brain . . .' Lester chewed on his spectacles

thoughtfully. 'Perhaps it was out of the heart . . . But anyway going to the brain meant he was finished.'

'But he was in hospital . . .'

'That was only a few days, thankfully. Terrible few days. He couldn't move. Couldn't eat. The brain must have turned to vegetable . . . '

Peter shifted uncomfortably in his seat. 'You mean Thurai who was in the Sakura Corporation?'

Lal Weerasinghe, the most assured and alert of our small party, nodded. He was a young man who moved in high circles and had a job in government as an economic adviser; he always sat forward on the edge of his seat. I never found out what his link with Peter was but he was very attentive.

Peter moved the conversation on. 'So, when are you fellows going to sort out this damn war?' But before anyone could answer he exploded into a violent cough again. His tongue stuck out and tears streamed down his cheeks. He put his hand up to his face and covered his nose and mouth letting his eyelids slowly drop over his eyes. I watched him closely; when the attack stopped he was hardly breathing. His breath was so shallow that his collar hardly moved.

Anton diverted us with the revolutionaries. 'Trouble is now these other buggers are playing up, no.'

'What, in the south?'

'But at the moment that is a problem for those who have something to hide. Corruption after all is also very bad . . . '

'Wipe them out.'

'Where's the money? We need to pay for an army up north, down south, buy ammunition . . . ' Lal Weerasinghe pulled back his sleeves and showed an empty hand.

Peter who had said nothing since he started to cough slowly began to struggle out of his chair. His grey

blubbery face changed colour like the monsoon sky. First
dark with a cloud of blood, then pale as the blood
drained into his stubby hands gripping the arms of his
chair.

'Never mind,' he mumbled. The phlegm in his throat
was like a cloth over a microphone. He tried to clear his
throat, but it was clearly a temporary measure in a
lifelong struggle against a steadily rising tide. Each time
he coughed there seemed to be a little less respite.

He stepped unsteadily towards the window mumbling
some more under his breath. His movement took
everyone by surprise. All our eyes were on him. At one
point he almost fell but a lamp stand saved him. He
turned around sheepishly and smiled at us.

No one said anything. We waited for some signal from
the maestro to start afresh, but he just stared out of the
window at the moon.

When he finally turned around he seemed back to
normal. 'Why is no one talking? This is a party . . . Come
on. Drinks? Let's hear some voices.'

Dinner was eventually served at about ten-thirty downstairs in the huge dining room. Chandrani came and
announced that the food was ready and we made our way
down. Peter shepherded us from the back, 'Go down, go
down,' he said without moving at all.

There were mountains of rice, tempered in butter and
sprinkled with cloves and cardamoms, and a sea of red
crabs. Dozens of other smaller dishes dotted the massive
round tamarind table. We sat down carefully leaving a
large chair free for Peter. He had not followed us.
Someone called out for him and there was a muffled
answer. Again we waited in silence for his signal, his
arrival.

Eventually he came down with slow, deliberate, quiet steps. He sat down on his chair and urged us to start. He called out for Chandrani to serve. His voice was tired and the words ran into each other, but he had carried down a fresh glass of whisky topped with soda up to the brim without spilling a drop. I wanted to reach over and slip it away from him, to save him. I felt he needed to stay alert. But he looked up at me as if he had read something more critical in my mind. *No, don't touch it.*

We began to eat praising the food and people started to talk about other parties, their overlapping lives.

'We never have those garden parties anymore do we?' Shiromi asked. 'At one time they seemed to happen every week almost.'

'Oh yes, those evening dos . . . '

'Uncle, do you remember you used to have those parties with Chinese bucket lanterns and oil lamps all over the garden?'

Peter who had been nodding off jerked up his head and stared around the table. Shiromi repeated her question.

'Yes,' he said. 'Yes. But there are too many mosquitoes now.'

A small ripple of laughter went round the table. Kamala Weerasinghe put her hands on the table. 'Anyway who has gardens these days? No one can afford them, never mind the party!'

'Anyone who has a garden has to build on it, that's the only way the children will have somewhere near to live. Who can do anything else?'

'Such a shame!'

'But what's to be done? There's no room otherwise. People will have to live on top of each other.'

Peter lifted his eyes as if puzzled by something, then he looked back down at his plate.

It was almost midnight when coffee was served. Peter pushed his cup aside, but others were grateful for it.

'Uncle you hardly ate anything!' Shiromi said.

Peter waved his hand.

'But you need to eat. It's not good otherwise.'

Peter shook his head slowly in a stupor.

As he finished the coffee Lester yawned loudly and said, 'Well, thank you Peter. Excellent dinner!'

There was a chorus of approval. Then people got up and starting making their way towards the door.

'Good night Uncle, good show.'

'Goodbye, fine party.'

Anton was the last to go. 'Good night! Just let me know if there's anything you need . . . ' he said looking at me.

Peter saw them all off without moving from the table. His mouth was drooping like his eyes. I stayed on feeling somehow responsible for seeing the whole thing through. They had all been asked over because of me, I thought. I also felt worried again as I had earlier in the evening when Peter had disappeared for his bath.

After the last of them had gone Peter dipped his fingers in a finger-bowl and squeezed the slice of lime floating in it. Then he wiped his hands on the towel that Chandrani had left on the table. 'Help me back upstairs to my chair,' he said to me.

I said I thought he ought to go to bed.

He looked at me terribly hurt. 'You think I have drunk too much too, like the rest of them.' He shook his head sadly.

I protested. 'No, no. But you look tired. It's been a long day.'

'Not long enough,' he said. 'Take me upstairs. You can have a night-cap.'

I went over to him and took his arm.

'No, my legs are asleep. Lift me!'

I put my hands under his arms and pulled. He was difficult to support; there was no frame beneath the suit. It was like trying to hold an enormous balloon of water. There was nothing I could get a grip on. He kept slipping out of my hands. I called out to Chandrani but she didn't come. In the end I bent down and got my shoulder in under his arm and levered him out. I tried to get his legs moving but they seemed so small and puny under that formless bulk. Slowly we managed to roll up the stairs pulling and pushing each other and then finally back on to the swivel-chair by the desk.

'Did you like the party?' he asked me in a hoarse voice when he was settled.

I said I did and thanked him for the evening.

'It's nothing. They'd come anytime for a free feed. Did you like the crabs? No flesh, no? I told you, it's the wrong time of the month—*poya*. Temple day.' He looked up at me looking for something. He lit yet another cigarette. The whites of his eyes were yellow and marbled with fine red veins. 'You know I really wanted to be a monk. I told you didn't I? A *monk*. Give up everything you know?' He looked down and noticed some rice grains on his silk tie. He flicked them off and smoothed the tie back down on the high curve of his stomach. His mouth collapsed in an awkward smile. He held the cigarette to it and panted; his breath let out a thin trail of smoke that slowly spread out above him, ascending.

Romesh Gunesekera grew up in Sri Lanka and the Philippines, and now lives in London. His first novel, *Reef,* was a finalist for the Booker Prize and was nominated for a New Voice Award. *Monkfish Moon* was a *New York Times* Notable Book of the Year.